"Sunny, what have you been doing—" Running around in the rain, Kale was about to say . . . until he saw her body beautifully revealed beneath the soaked shirt.

Her face was lit with a smile so dazzling it nearly drove away the summer squall. And her skin shimmered through the drenched fabric and stole all rational thought from his brain. He reached out to caress her, to touch the erotic vision that offered itself to his hands.

Then his conscience told him to put his hand in his pocket, the girl in the car, and his libido on hold. His id told his conscience to take a hike. But he could no more resist the temptation of Sunny's lush lips than a cobra could resist the charmer's flute.

"Tell me to stop," he said huskily.

She looked up at him with big blue eyes. "Why should I do that?" She moved closer to him. "It's what I want."

With a groan he captured her mouth and lifted her close against him. He wanted to rip off her clothes, lay her down on the sand, and make love to her while the surf rolled over them. . . .

WHAT ARE *LOVESWEPT* ROMANCES?

They are stories of true romance and touching emotion. We believe those two very important ingredients are constants in our highly sensual and very believable stories in the *LOVESWEPT* line. Our goal is to give you, the reader, stories of consistently high quality that may sometimes make you laugh, sometimes make you cry, but are always fresh and creative and contain many delightful surprises within their pages.

Most romance fans read an enormous number of books. Those they truly love, they keep. Others may be traded with friends and soon forgotten. We hope that each *LOVESWEPT* romance will be a treasure—a "keeper." We will always try to publish

LOVE STORIES YOU'LL NEVER FORGET
BY AUTHORS YOU'LL ALWAYS REMEMBER

The Editors

Jan Hudson
Sunny Says

BANTAM BOOKS
NEW YORK · TORONTO · LONDON · SYDNEY · AUCKLAND

SUNNY SAYS

A Bantam Book / December 1992

*If you would be interested in receiving protective vinyl
covers for your Loveswept books, please write to this address
for information:*

Loveswept
Bantam Books
P.O. Box 985
Hicksville, NY 11802

ISBN 0-553-44090-X

Published simultaneously in the United States and Canada

*Bantam Books are published by Bantam Books, a division of
Bantam Doubleday Dell Publishing Group, Inc. Its trademark,
consisting of the words "Bantam Books" and the portrayal of
a rooster, is Registered in U.S. Patent and Trademark Office
and in other countries. Marca Registrada. Bantam Books, 666
Fifth Avenue, New York, New York 10103.*

PRINTED IN THE UNITED STATES OF AMERICA

OPM   0 9 8 7 6 5 4 3 2 1

Thanks to Alan Moller, Patti Barricklow, and Peggy Cleaves for information that made my life easier.

Special thanks also to Dr. Neil Frank, meteorologist at KHOU-TV in Houston, and Sergeant Isaac Valencia of the Corpus Christi Police Department.

If I've made any technical errors, the fault is entirely mine and not that of these fine folks who tried to educate me.

One

Hulon Eubanks was threatening to jump again. For the third time in the past two weeks, Sunny Larkin kicked off her high heels and climbed out onto the window ledge.

"Hang on, Hulon," she yelled to the anchorman who sat hunched against the concrete embrasure a few feet away. "I'm coming out."

"It's no use, Sunny. Nobody will listen to me." He hung his head. An August breeze from Corpus Christi Bay ruffled the strands of his salt-and-pepper hairpiece, which sat slightly askew. "Nobody cares that I'm miserable in this job. Nobody cares that I toss my cookies at five-forty-five every Monday through Friday."

"Oh, Hulon, that's not true." Crawling on her hands and knees and trying not to look down at the parking lot four floors below, Sunny swallowed back her anxiety and inched her way toward the middle-aged man in the green polka-dot tie. The breeze billowed her skirt, and the rough surface of the concrete molding abraded her kneecaps. She felt a run on her panty hose pop and slither along her leg.

Behind her in the KRIP-TV newsroom, phones rang, teletypes clacked, printers spit out stories, prebroadcast conversation hummed, and business went on as usual. No one gave the pair on the ledge more than a cursory glance.

Hulon narrowed his eyes. "Then where's Foster? Did you call him?"

"Of course I called him. He's . . . uh . . . tied up at the moment." She crossed her fingers and gave him one of her perkiest, most reassuring smiles. "But he . . . he promised that he'd be up to talk to you at the first opportunity." The general manager of the station hadn't used exactly those words. His had been considerably more colorful and a tad obscene.

Hulon Eubanks—whose distinguished visage and sonorous voice were recognized by most Corpus Christi, Texas, residents as those of the evening anchor of Channel 13, The Good News Station—rolled his eyes and gave a bitter, disbelieving snort. "Then I'll stay here until that *opportunity* arises. Or until I decide to jump." He plucked one of the makeup tissues tucked protectively around his shirt collar, held it out, then released it and watched the scrap of white flutter downward.

As if the tissue were a hypnotist's pendulum, its slow, drifting descent captured Sunny's gaze, and her eyes followed it down, down, down until it landed on the hard, black asphalt. She grew dizzy. Beads of perspiration popped out across her upper lip. She closed her eyes and drew in a deep breath.

"Hulon, please, please, come back inside. You

can't stay out here. It's going to start raining any minute, and you'll get soaked."

"Rain?" From their perch on the front of the Parrish Building, she watched as he frowned and scanned the area, past the gently swaying palm trees along Shoreline Drive and across to the downtown harbor, where gleaming yachts and tall-masted sailboats rested quietly in their slips. He craned his neck, looking upward to where only a few scattered puffs of cumulus clouds sat placidly in an otherwise clear sky. "I know you're always right, but— Oh, you're joshing me. No, I'm staying until Foster comes. But you go back inside, my dear."

"I'm not leaving you out here alone, and you know how I hate heights. I've already ruined a new pair of panty hose, and the way my stomach's feeling, I'll never last until five-forty-five to join you in upchucking."

After a moment's hesitation that seemed like eons to her, he sighed. "Very well. But only for you Sunny, my girl. Only for you."

She sagged with relief. Carefully, she eased backward toward the open window. A sudden gust of wind tossed her skirt over her head, and she tried to bat it down. Her knee slid off the ledge, and she screamed, scrambling for a hold. Her life passed before her eyes as she hooked her toes around the window frame and grabbed the mini-blind cord with both hands. Her foot slipped, the blinds zipped to the top, and she dangled over four stories of nothing.

"Sunny! Take my hand," Hulon shouted as fat raindrops began pelting them.

"Stay back, Hulon, or we'll both go. Get some help!"

Her heart rampaging like a Panhandle tornado,

she whimpered as her puny lifeline cut into her hands. Dear Lord, she couldn't die in such an ignominious way. Twenty-six was too young to end up as a mere splat on the pavement. She had dreams to fulfill, things to do, places to go, people to see. Echoes of local newscasters announcing her bizarre demise reverberated in her head. But at the same time another, stronger voice said, *Don't be such a pantywaist. You can't give up.*

A mottled gray-and-white sea gull swooped from the sky and settled on the ledge above her. He looked down at her, cocking his head back and forth and taunting her with beady eyes.

"Shoo! Shoo!"

Undaunted, he only waddled around in a awkward half circle and presented his backside. When he ruffled his tail feathers, Sunny glared up at him. "Don't . . . you . . . dare, you nasty bird!"

Still hanging on for dear life, she clenched her teeth and looped the cord around her fist. After a deep breath, she felt for the bricks with her toes. With raindrops battering her back, she began walking up the side of the building, pulling with her hands and looping the cord as she went.

The sea gull took off with a startling flap. Sunny's foot slipped, and she screamed as she swung away, legs pumping, suspended again in midair. She heard an ominous splintering sound overhead and felt the cord give.

She squeezed her eyes shut. *Don't look down. Don't look down,* she repeated over and over like a mantra. Where was her guardian angel when she needed him?

Strong fingers clamped around her wrists. "I've got you," a deep voice said. "Let go."

"Are you crazy?" she shrieked.

"Trust me," the calm, resonant voice said.

She opened one eye, then the other, and glanced up into the tanned, rough-planed features of a man who somehow seemed familiar. Familiar, yet she couldn't put a name to this somber rescuer whose stubbled face said he'd seen it all, battled the world's vagaries and survived. His hazel eyes bored into hers with a palpable intensity that permeated every petrified cell in her body. A peculiar, soothing energy flowed from his callused hands to her wrists and washed over her.

"Trust me," he repeated slowly. "Let go."

Instinctively, she obeyed his directive. She would follow this man anywhere.

With a deft yank, he pulled her inside.

When her feet touched the floor, she fell against her lifesaver and flung her arms around him. Her face pressing against his chest, her fingers clutching handfuls of fabric at his back, she clung to him like a child terrorized by a nightmare.

He held her close, not speaking but exuding a raw strength and sense of security that was rock solid and infinitely reassuring. She burrowed closer, luxuriating in the safe port of his arms until she gradually gained control of her wobbly knees and racing heart.

When she was calm enough to think, it dawned on her that she was standing in the newsroom, the focus of a score of curious eyes, and clinging to a stranger like a frightened monkey. She looked up at him. Though it was a mere flash, an unspoken communication, both potent and elemental, passed between them. It jolted her like forked lightning. Her solar plexus swirled in that peculiar way which, if she hadn't known better, forewarned of an impending hurricane. Yet this time the feeling was vaguely different, more . . . poignant, more sensual. Shaken, she laughed nervously and stepped away from him.

"Whew! That was a close call," she said, running her hand over her short cap of damp blond hair. She gave her savior the biggest, most dazzling smile she could muster and stuck her hand out. "Thanks. I thought I was a goner."

Feet planted apart and fists rammed against the hips of his rumpled bush jacket, he glared at her. "What in the hell were you doing out there?"

Her smile faded, and her hand dropped. His scowl deepened the sun- and life-lined creases at the corners of his eyes and across his forehead. From her five-foot-three vantage point, his six feet of sinew seemed suddenly menacing. "I—I—"

He bent over and stuck his face in hers. "Don't you know you could have broken your damned neck?"

Her eyebrow shot up, and her spine stiffened. She held her ground and glared at him, nose to nose. "Who stepped on your tail, Mr. Congeniality? *I'm* the one who was at the mercy of the mini-blinds."

Except for a slight upward twitch at the corner of his mouth, neither of them moved a muscle.

Foster Dunn, KRIP's well-manicured general manager, rushed over and threw an arm around each of them. "Now, now, we'll sort this out later. The important thing is that Sunny's safe. You *are* okay?" he asked her.

Splaying a hand across the bodice of her damp sailor dress, she drew in a deep breath. "I'm fine."

"Good, good." He patted her shoulder. "Back to work, everybody. The excitement is over. Sunny's fine."

"I still want to know why in the hell she was hanging out the window," her rescuer growled.

Her eyes narrowed. "I'm practicing to become a cat burglar."

"Now, now," Foster repeated. "Let's forget about it." The general manager, who hated confrontations of any sort, straightened the vest of his pin-striped suit and tugged his cuffs into place. "Sunny, this is my cousin Kale Hoaglin, the new co-owner of KRIP. He's just flown in from an assignment in Bangladesh. Sunny Larkin is our weathergirl. And a damned fine one she is," he added affably. "Isn't she just as cute as a bug?"

"Weather *reporter*," Sunny amended automatically. As the rest of Foster's words sunk in, she felt the blood drain from her face, aghast that she'd been insulting *the* Kale Hoaglin, one of the world's most famous foreign correspondents. She and the majority of the female population had drooled over him for years. Of course, he looked a bit scruffier in person than he did on the network news. He hadn't shaved in several days. His thick shock of light brown hair was overlong, sun-streaked, and looked as if he'd run his fingers through it a thousand times. Plus he must have slept in his clothes.

"Forgive me," she said. "I should've recognized you at once. It's an honor to meet such a renowned newsman." She offered her hand, and this time he took it. "Your aunt Ravinia talked about you all the time. Please accept my condolences. We all loved Ravinia and were devastated by her death. I'll miss her."

"Although I didn't see her much in the past few years, I'll miss her too," Kale said, a shadow further darkening his solemnity. "She was . . . unique."

"Unique" was a mild term for Ravinia Irene Parrish, Sunny thought. Not that she was one to throw stones. Sunny herself had been called worse. Perhaps that's why the two women, despite the disparity in their ages, had formed an instant affinity. She truly would miss the eccentric owner of KRIP, but at least when Ravinia's time came up she'd died with panache. Two weeks before, Ravinia's plane had crashed in the Himalayas. The only remains were ashes, a few pieces of twisted metal, and, miraculously, the gold ankh she always wore. Sunny noticed that the Egyptian symbol of life now hung in the opening of Kale's wrinkled pink shirt.

A childless widow, Ravinia had left everything to her two nephews, Kale Hoaglin and Foster Dunn. The station had been abuzz with speculations about KRIP's fate. Foster and Ravinia had rarely agreed about anything, especially local programming. His aunt had always dismissed his objections with a chuck of his cheek, a lilting laugh, an imperious flutter of fingers flashing with the oversized rings she favored. "Humor an old lady," she'd said to those who challenged her unconventional ideas. "My way is more fun, and I can afford to indulge my foibles." Then she'd be off, trailing a cloud of Shalimar, on her way to attend yoga class, to care for her bromeliads, or to jet to San Francisco for an AIDS benefit or Paris for the spring showings.

Sunny doubted that the dour Kale Hoaglin would be content with Ravinia's broadcasting philosophies either. She suspected that the veteran hard-line newsman would instigate some massive changes.

Hulon Eubanks cleared his throat. Foster introduced him to Kale, clapping him on the back and saying, "Hulon here has been filling in as news director and anchorman since we lost our last one a couple of months ago."

"And I need to speak with you about my position, Foster. You, too, Mr. Hoaglin."

"Later, Hulon, later," Foster said, brushing him aside and steering Kale toward Estella Jones's desk. "I'd like for you to meet our sportscaster."

When the beautiful coffee-skinned woman stood, Sunny stifled a giggle at Kale's gaping expression. Estella was very tall, towering two inches over Kale with her heels on, and very, very pregnant.

Before she laughed out loud, Sunny fled to the lounge to make the repairs needed for the evening telecast. She changed into a spare outfit she kept at the station, tended the damage to her hair, and was applying the heavier cosmetics needed on camera when Estella Jones strolled in.

"Well, roomie," Estella said, easing her cumbersome body into the next chair at the long makeup mirror, "what do you think of our new boss?"

Sunny shrugged and continued applying her lipstick.

The tall woman, who was Sunny's best friend and housemate, laughed and reached for a powder puff. "For a moment there, I thought I was watching the reunion of soul mates."

"What in the world are you talking about?"

"I'm talking about you and Kale Hoaglin. I'm talking about enough sparks to kindle a bonfire. Honey, I'm talking about enough signals to alert the entire Pacific fleet."

"That's the craziest thing I've ever heard of. I think Ed's been gone too long." Lieutenant Edward Jones, Estella's husband and a navy pilot, was on a six-month tour of duty on an aircraft carrier.

Estella stroked her rounded belly. "It *has* been a

long time, but I've seen that look in Ed's eyes too many times not to recognize it."

"You're imagining things. Why, the man was furious with me. That's what you saw. I thought he was going to eat me alive."

A slow grin spread over Estella's face. "Uh-huh."

Kale sat in Foster's plush office watching the six o'clock news with his cousin. As Hulon droned on about one of the seemingly endless pieces of fluff that was supposed to pass for local news, Kale rubbed his eyes and yawned. "I knew I was tired," he said, "but this crap would put anybody to sleep."

Foster nodded. "Now you know why KRIP is in the cellar of local ratings. We can't even sell advertising to the Boy Scouts. When Aunt Ravinia came up with this absurd idea, I tried to tell her that nobody wanted to hear only good news. It's dull. The public likes blood and sensationalism, murder and mayhem, conflict and chaos. Perhaps it's a sad indictment of human nature, but it's true."

Kale rubbed his forehead, thinking that Foster's ideas seemed to be as extreme as Ravinia's. "At least people deserve to be informed. News can't be a series of human-interest stories. And Eubanks can't even make those sound interesting. The man looks as if he's in pain." He glanced back at the set where Estella was extolling the charitable deeds of a National League pitcher. Kale groaned. "Unbelievable. Where did Ravinia dig this one up? Big Bird would have more credibility. And why in the hell isn't she reporting the baseball scores?"

"I think Ravinia met Estella in yoga class. Actually her credentials aren't bad, but when I complained about this segment, our dear auntie said that reporting sports scores condoned competition. 'Imagine how the poor losers feel, darling,' were her words, as I recall."

Kale groaned again.

"Now do you understand why I pleaded with you to come? Half of KRIP is yours, and I can't get this mess straightened out by myself," Foster said.

"The place is a zoo. The easiest thing to do would be to fire everybody and start from scratch."

"Can't. What you see is what we've got to work with. Ravinia renegotiated everybody's contract two months ago—with raises, I might add. Except for Sunny." Foster nodded toward the screen.

"Ah, our daring Little Miss Sunshine. Is she holding out for pitons and a grappling hook?"

"Not exactly." Foster squirmed in his chair.

Kale watched as Sunny recounted the day's weather, using the latest in colorful graphics. In her well-modulated voice, she reported the high and low temperatures. Given her perky, cheerleader looks, he'd been expecting a cutesy, saccharine performance, but he was surprised. She seemed knowledgeable and professional as she described upper-level troughs and low-pressure systems. In fact, she had a phenomenal TV presence.

He leaned closer, captivated. Her big blue eyes sparkled with life, and her deep dimples flashed as she related the water temperature off Padre Island. Kale grew fascinated with her cap of pale blond hair, wondering if it felt as silky as it looked. Her blouse curved enticingly as she pointed out a patch of thunderstorms on radar, and he stirred, remembering how those soft curves had felt when he'd held her against him.

"She's good," Kale said. "Damned good."

Foster nodded. "Would you believe that the last five-minute segment of the show is the only thing that's keeping us alive? People watch news on the other channels in town, then switch to Sunny for the weather report."

Puzzled, Kale said, "That's strange. I mean, she far outclasses the rest of the tripe on KRIP, but, hell, one weather report is pretty much like another."

"We-ll, not exactly. Watch."

"And for tomorrow's weather, the National Weather Service predicts continued cloudiness with an eighty percent chance of rain. But Sunny says"—she paused to beam a golden smile that charmed the camera and bored into Kale's midsection—"the skies will clear before dawn, and tomorrow is going to be a bright, sunshiny day with highs in the mid-nineties, so don't forget your sunscreen."

"Good God!" Kale exploded. "Why did she have to blow it with that outlandish prediction? Is the woman nuts?"

Foster punched off the program with the remote control and stood. "Sounds crazy, but she's always right."

Dumbfounded, Kale stared at his cousin. "What the hell are you talking about? How can that slip of a girl know more than the National Weather Service?"

Foster shrugged. "Beats me. I think it has something to do with her left ear itching."

"Her *ear*? Holy hell! Now I've heard it all. Our crazy aunt has turned this station into a damned sideshow!" Kale shot out of his chair and strode to the door. "I'm going to Ravinia's house, down a double shot of Scotch, and fall into bed. After I've had about two days of sleep, maybe I can deal with this mess. But not now."

"Before you leave, there's something I should warn—"

Kale slammed the door on his cousin's words and stalked out of the building, muttering curses and deprecations that would have melted the strings of Ravinia's harp if she'd been listening. How in the hell, in the two weeks vacation he'd scheduled, could he even begin to bring order to this chaos? It sickened him to think that KRIP, once the top-rated TV news station of Corpus Christi and the surrounding area, had turned into a bad joke.

Kale awoke feeling muzzy-headed and disoriented. In the dim light of the drapery-darkened room, he squinted at the furnishings, trying to get his bearings. Lord knows, in the past eight years he'd awakened in an endless array of strange places, most of them dirty and dangerous. When he caught the scents of potpourri and lemon oil and recognized the heavy Victorian furniture, he relaxed on his pillow and glanced at the ceiling. His old Farrah Fawcett pinup poster, curled around the edges now, was still there, a familiar relic from the years when he spent summers in this room and worked at KRIP in its heyday.

He yawned, stretched, and scratched his belly, thinking he couldn't remember when he'd had such a relaxed night's rest. He'd been so tired the evening before, he'd merely stripped and dropped into the big bed. How long had he slept? He checked his watch. Twelve hours. It was seven A.M. on Saturday. He listened to the muffled patter of rain and considered drifting back to sleep.

Rain? Sounded like Little Miss Sunshine blew it. A shame, in a way, but not surprising. Thoughts of Sunny brought a blurry recollection of his having dreamt about her, something vaguely erotic. He tried to recapture the fleeting remnant, but it was gone.

Damn! What was it about Sunny Larkin that hooked his attention, stirred him, made him feel . . . protective? Was it her bright smile that tugged at him? Maybe it was the sweet sort of innocence that shone from her big blue eyes, a sassy naïveté that was missing in the eyes of the women he'd encountered in the squalid, disaster-riddled places he'd been lately.

Or maybe it was simply her cute little tush that reminded him that he'd been a long time without a woman. He threw back the covers and headed for the bathroom, eager to shed the grime he'd toted halfway around the world.

Sunny stood under the pulsating spray, humming softly and lathering her body with herb-scented soap. With a sudden, clattering swish, the shower curtain flew open. Her heart jumped to her throat, and her eyes widened in shock.

A naked man stood glowering at her. She screamed bloody murder.

Two

Sunny whipped the shower curtain around her like a sarong. "What are you doing here?" She tried desperately to keep her eyes on Kale Hoaglin's scowling face and ignore the other impressive parts of his anatomy, which he seemed to have no interest in covering. Had the man no shame?

"This is *my* house. And I'm about to take a shower in *my* bathroom. The question is, what are *you* doing here?"

"I live here. That is, *we* live here. I mean, Estella and I have been house-sitting for Ravinia. After her death, Foster asked us to stay on and—what are you staring at?" she asked.

"The interesting array of polka dots."

She looked down at the widely spaced, dime-sized dots decorating the clear curtain. They afforded about as much coverage as a fly's wing. Her face blazed. She spun around, presenting her back to him and still gathering the transparent plastic to her with as much dignity as she could summon.

"Mr. Hoaglin, if you'll step out for a moment, please, I'll leave."

"Don't you think that 'Mr. Hoaglin' seems a little too formal for the situation?" he asked, stepping into the tub beside her. "Call me Kale." He tugged at the curtain clutched in her hands.

"What are you *doing*?" she shrieked.

"Taking a shower." He held out the soap to her. "Mind washing my back?"

She snatched the soap and flung it. The bar caromed off the tile wall and fell into the tub with a dull thud. "Wash your own back, you pervert!" She scrambled from the tub, grabbed a towel, and hurried to her bedroom, slamming the door to the connecting bath so hard that the pictures jiggled on the wall.

When she heard deep laughter from the bathroom, she itched to throw open the door and give him a blistering set-down. Instead, she took a deep breath, counted to ten, and reminded herself that Kale Hoaglin was her boss. And, after all, this *was* his house.

By the time she'd dressed, Sunny's temper had cooled, but her embarrassment lingered. Her steps didn't have their usual spring as she went downstairs to fix breakfast. How did she always seem to land in such messes? Not only had she already had two humiliating experiences with Kale, but now that he was here, she and Estella would have no option but to vacate the lovely old estate they'd called home for the past several months. With Estella's advanced pregnancy, finding a new place and moving would present a problem.

Too bad they would have to leave, she thought, staring out the kitchen window across Ocean Drive. She loved the view overlooking the water.

Only the palm-lined boulevard and a curving grassy bluff beyond it separated the stately stone mansion from the magnificent panorama of the Gulf inlet. If Corpus Christi, which hugged the bay with cupped hands, was often called "The Sparkling City by the Sea," surely this spot was one of the diamonds on its finger.

And she and Estella certainly wouldn't be able to afford the housekeeper who came three times a week. But then, she and Estella didn't have truckloads of priceless furniture and doodads that needed polishing either.

She started the coffee and downed a glass of orange juice as though it were a shot of red-eye. Maybe when the vitamin C kicked in, she'd be able to think more clearly about options. Something would turn up. It always did. No need to sweat the small stuff.

As for the encounter in the shower with her new boss, it was no big deal, she convinced herself. She'd grown up with three brothers and two sisters who shared one bathroom, and modesty had been a lost cause. Too, thinking back on it, the situation had been sort of funny.

Soon she was whistling as she bustled about the huge old kitchen, and her whole body bounced to the tune as she rhythmically plopped spoonfuls of pancake batter on the griddle.

"Could I have a cup of that coffee?" asked a deep voice from behind her.

Startled, Sunny jerked, and a big dollop of batter flew over her shoulder. She whirled around to find Kale standing there, a glob of goo sliding slowly down his cheek.

He stood still as a statue, his face expressionless except for a tiny twitch in his jaw. "A simple no would have sufficed."

She tried to keep a straight face, to act contrite, but a bubble of laughter exploded in her throat. He glared. Another bubble escaped, then another. She gritted her teeth to hold back the gales threatening to erupt and grabbed a paper towel.

"Sorry about that." She quickly wiped the batter away.

"Why do I get the feeling that you're not at all sorry?"

She wet another towel and scrubbed the vestiges from his cheek, noticing that it was clean shaven now. Smiling, she cocked her head and looked up at him, about to say something glib. Their eyes locked like dueling sabers. Her thoughts fled. Her smile faded. Her strokes lapsed into slow motion, then stopped. The intensity of his gaze was so potent that she could have sworn he had X-ray vision and was scrutinizing the synapses in her brain.

A shiver akin to what she felt with an approaching thunderstorm slithered up her spine. She blinked, breaking the disquieting contact between them, and hurriedly returned to the pancakes.

He poured a mug of coffee and, while he sipped it, lifted the ruffled curtain over the sink and peered out. "I could have sworn that I heard it raining a few minutes ago."

"Nope. The weather cleared about five this morning. It's going to be a beautiful day."

"Must have been the shower I heard."

Her hand stilled as she scooped pancakes onto a platter. "Probably." She kept her eyes averted while she finished her task. "Would you like some of these?" She waved her hand over the heaped dish.

"They look better than anything I've seen in weeks. Do you have enough for me?"

"Oh, sure. I can't possibly eat all these, and Estella's are already in the warming drawer. I come from a big family, and I can't seem to break the habit of cooking too much. All my recipes are for eight, and even when I halve them . . ." She shrugged. "Orange juice and strawberries are in the fridge. Everything else is on the table. You can have Estella's place. She won't be up for an hour or two."

They carried the food to a breakfast nook where baskets of greenery hung in the corners and pots of bromeliads lined the ledge of a huge bay window overlooking the lush backyard. Morning sun shimmered across the swimming pool's blue reflection. A breeze rippled the water, waved the leaves of the banana trees, rustled the palm fronds, and set the huge red blossoms of hibiscus bushes nodding.

"I'd forgotten how much I like it here. It's so peaceful, so clean." After a moment his gaze turned to her with that fierce, penetrating scrutiny that gripped her like a fisherman's gaff. "And the view is spectacular." His forehead wrinkled. "How did you know?"

"Know what?"

"That it wasn't going to rain today."

"I just knew." Sunny grabbed the glass bottle shaped like a grandmother and thrust it toward Kale. "Have some syrup."

With the bottle hovering over his pancakes, he paused and stared down at his plate. He frowned as if trying to decipher hieroglyphics.

Sunny reached across and rotated his plate a quarter turn until the design on the pancakes was facing him. "It's a happy face made of raisins and cherry slices."

When he raised one eyebrow in a you've-got-to-be-kidding gesture, she shrugged and said, "Estella needs cheering up these days. Just pick them out if they bother you."

She busied herself spooning strawberries into bowls and pouring orange juice, trying to act blasé and to disregard Kale's looming presence, which charged the air around him. "Listen, I'm really sorry about Estella's and my intrusion on your privacy here. Ravinia insisted that we move in with her. I think she worried about Estella being alone and pregnant, and although her excuse was that she needed us to house-sit while she was out of town, she really wasn't gone all that often. I believe she was more lonely than anything. Anyway, if you'll give me a couple of days, I'll find another place for us to live, and we'll be gone."

"No need for that. We can manage for the short time I'll be here. Until Foster and I decide what to do with the place, you'd be doing us a favor by continuing to watch out for things here."

"Well," she said, hesitating as she considered the range of complications of both staying and going, "I suppose we can stay, at least until the baby is born and Estella's husband returns from his sea duty. Neither you nor Foster wants to live in the house permanently?" she asked.

He shook his head. "I live out of a suitcase most of the time. And can you imagine Foster and Alicia living here with their two little hellions?"

Sunny chuckled. "Alicia doesn't seem the type to appreciate a moose head over the fireplace, a suit of armor in the hall, and a collection of blowguns and tomahawks on the wall. And Ravinia's bromeliads would all be dead with a week."

Kale nodded. "I imagine their kids could trash Ravinia's accumulation of Greek and Chinese artifacts in two days." They ate silently for a few moments, then he stared at her again, his eyes narrowed. "Is it true that you're never wrong about the weather?"

"'Rarely' would be more accurate."

"How rarely?"

She sighed, not wanting to discuss the subject. "I've missed once or twice."

Stone-faced, he continued to pin her with his gaze. "Once or twice?" he asked skeptically.

"Well, once. I was coming down with the flu." What was it about this man that made her nervous enough to jump through her skin? "Are you finished?" She reached for his plate, eager to evade his line of questioning and flee the room.

His hand clamped her wrist. "No, I'm not finished. These pancakes are the best thing I've eaten in a long time, and I plan to devour every crumb."

He continued to eat, seemingly absorbed in his food, but his left hand remained around her wrist. She tried to gently tug away, but he held on firmly and his thumb absently stroked the tendons along the back of her hand.

She felt heat radiate under her chin, and tiny prickles tingled her scalp. Was he coming on to her? No, surely it was her imagination. She tugged again. He held firm. Seductive currents rippled up her arm and swirled inside her like a building cyclone. She had a feeling she'd made a *big* mistake in agreeing to stay in the same house with Kale Hoaglin, even for a couple of weeks. Oh, he was a sexy devil all right, and under different circumstances she'd be attracted to him, but she had no intention of being a temporary diversion for someone who'd simply been in Bangladesh too long.

When his thumb made slow forays between her

fingers, she sucked in a breath, jerked her wrist back, and jumped up. "Listen, Mr. Hoaglin, I think we'd better get one thing straight right now. I don't come as a bed warmer with the house. Our relationship must be strictly professional. Maybe I'm mistaking your intentions, but if you try to hit on me, I'll scream sexual harassment so loudly that reporters will be on your tail before sundown."

He looked at her as if she'd lost her mind. "I don't know what in the hell you're talking about. If I meant to *hit* on you, sweetheart, you wouldn't mistake my intentions." His eyes raked her from toe to crown. "You can relax. You're not my type."

A wave of humiliation flooded her. She ached to shrivel into a dust ball on the floor. Besides feeling totally mortified, she felt oddly . . . bereft. Refusing to examine the latter response too closely, she brazened the situation out with a saucy grin and a waggle of her head. "Good. I've never pictured myself as a groupie for a network stud."

She restrained a giggle when she saw that her zinger had gone straight to his molars. His expression turned as icy as a Canadian cold front.

"That was a cheap shot. I resent the hell out of that label. I was out busting my butt to become a serious journalist when you were still in training bras."

"Oh, lighten up, Hoaglin. Don't be such a bear," she said, laughing. Not even a smidgeon of a smile appeared on his lips. Holding her hands prayerfully beneath her chin, she bowed. "Forgive me, your venerableness, I didn't mean to rattle your slats. Why don't we call the score tied and start over? Pretty please?"

Looking her up and down as solemnly as an embalmer eyeing a corpse, he waited a long time before answering. Then he gave a curt nod. "Fair enough."

Quickly gathering the dishes from the table, Sunny said, "If you'll excuse me, I'll just stick these in the dishwasher and be off. I'm a working girl."

"On Saturday?"

"Yep. I get to be both reporter and anchor for tonight's news. My contribution is to cover some sort of do that the historical society is having this morning."

"Sounds deadly dull," he said, following her into the kitchen.

"Probably. But Ravinia's good-news policy puts the quietus on all the interesting stuff."

"That policy is about to change."

"Well, hallelujah! It's not a moment too soon." Sunny wiped her hands and tossed the dish towel on the counter. "Everybody on the staff has been about to go crazy with the good-news business. I adored Ravinia, but sometimes she got the strangest ideas. I think the good-news concept was something her guru conned her into. Everybody except your aunt could see that it wasn't working. People like a little excitement in their lives."

"Even you?"

She laughed. "Especially me. Have you ever seen a news reporter worth his or her salt who didn't thrive on excitement?"

"But I thought you were a weathergirl, not a newsperson."

"Weather *reporter*," she said, her irritation with the term shading her words. "And the weather can be exciting sometimes, especially when a hurricane howls into the Gulf. But I don't intend to spend my life doing the weather. I have bigger plans in mind."

"Oh?" He looked faintly amused—at least that's what she surmised from the faint movement of his lips. It was hard to read a face that was about as animated as those of the Mount Rushmore quartet.

"Believe it. I have a real nose for news. Connie Chung and Diane Sawyer had better move over and make room for Sunny Larkin," she said, laughing and giving an exaggerated strut as she left the kitchen.

She thought she heard a snort behind her, but she ignored it. She wasn't about to let some sourpuss cynic rain on her parade, even if he was a high-profile muckety-muck with the network. He simply didn't know how determined she was to reach the goals she'd set for herself.

In the entry hall, she headed for the table Ravinia had acquired the year before. The table, standing in the center of the impressive foyer, was big and circular with a mosaic top of polished malachite and a base formed by three large elephants intricately carved from some sort of exotic wood.

Sunny picked up her shoulder bag from the table and searched for her keys. They were missing. She knelt on the floor and peered amid the legs. "Dumbo, did you eat my keys?"

"Who's Dumbo?" Kale asked from behind her.

She stroked the tummy of one of the elephants. "This fellow. Estella and I dubbed this piece 'Dumbo and Friends,' but Ravinia thought the table was divine, a true work of art. I suppose it is. I understand that a couple of museums bid against her. Some guy on a mountain somewhere spent his entire life creating this thing." She shrugged. "To each his own, I suppose." She patted around under the table.

"Looking for these?" Kale jingled a set of keys in front of him.

Sunny jumped up and grabbed them. "Where did you find them?"

"In the refrigerator beside the strawberries."

"I wonder how they got there." She shrugged. "Oh, well. I'm off to work. See you later." She waved as she hurried out.

Kale followed her to the driveway. "Mind if I ride along?"

"I'm not going directly to the station. I brought home one of the KRIP vans, and I'm meeting Carlos at the heritage society do."

"Who's Carlos?"

"Carlos Mondragon. He's my crew."

"A one-person crew?"

Sunny laughed. "Foster put us on a strict budget. I can drop you off at the station if you'd like. Or you can drive Ravinia's car. It's in the garage."

"I think I'll tag along with you. I can't remember when I've been to a heritage society do." He looked down at his clothes. "Think I'm dressed appropriately?"

Was he actually joking with her? She scanned his face for any sign of a smile, but there was none. She glanced at the pink shirt and chinos he wore. They were considerably cleaner and slightly less rumpled than the clothes he'd had on the day before. "I think you'll pass. Corpus is a pretty informal place."

"Want me to drive?" he asked.

"Nope. It'll do you good to relinquish control for a few minutes. Climb in."

After they had pulled away, Kale scowled at her. "What did you mean by that 'control' remark?"

"Sorry, boss, but you strike me as the type who

likes to be in charge. If I'm wrong, accept my apology."

"Apology accepted. And cut out that 'boss' stuff. You make me feel ancient."

"Right, boss—I mean, Kale. And I haven't worn training bras since I was twelve. That's fourteen years ago. By the way, since we have plenty of time, I hope you don't mind that I need to run a couple of errands on the way."

He cocked an eyebrow. "Personal business on company time?"

Was he teasing her? Who could tell with his perpetually grim expression? "The *company* van needs gas," she shot back. "And," she added with a saucy grin, "since I have only two dollars and six cents in my purse, I have to stop by the ATM at the bank. You gonna fire me, boss?"

"Not unless you rear-end that Buick."

She slammed on her brakes. "I saw it."

"Ummm."

After they stopped for gas, which Kale insisted on pumping and paying for himself, they drove to the small branch bank where Sunny kept her account. As they pulled into the parking lot, she had an eerie feeling—not a weather feeling, but a general, more pervasive sensation, a news feeling that twitched her nose and put her on guard.

"Were you serious about a change in the news policy at KRIP?" she asked.

"Very."

"Then grab the camera from the back."

"Why?"

"I've got a funny—" A commotion erupted in front of the bank. "Robbery in progress!" she shouted.

As Kale reached for the video-cam, two men with paper bags ran from the bank. A guard at the door leveled his gun and fired as they scrambled for the backseat of a waiting car. A third robber, a watch cap pulled low over his eyes, stumbled, dropped his bag, then lifted his gun and fired at the guard. Two shots pinged off the archway pier the guard used for cover.

When the robber reached for the paper bag, Sunny floorboarded the van. "Hang on," she yelled at Kale, who was halfway out the window shooting the scene. She rammed the getaway car from the rear.

The robber squeezed off a shot toward her, and a spiderweb cracked across the passenger side of the windshield. The holdup man threw himself in the front seat of the old Chevrolet Monte Carlo, and the car burned rubber, with the door still hanging open.

Sunny tore out behind him, shouting to Kale, "You okay?"

"I'm okay. Stop the van."

"Not on your life." She gripped the wheel and stomped the accelerator harder.

"Dammit! I said stop the van! You're going to get yourself killed."

"Forget it, Hoaglin. This is the lead story on KRIP tonight. Keep filming." She heard the distant whine of sirens and grabbed the mobile phone, punching in 911.

She stayed on the robbers' tail, squealing around corners, until another shot rang out. She dropped back but kept the car in sight until she could describe its route to the police. "It's an old maroon Monte Carlo. We're on Gollihar Road just past the Parkdale Plaza. Wait! They've just turned left on McGregor." She hung a left behind them.

Two white Corpus Christi Police Department Caprices—sirens screaming, lights flashing—

roared out from a side street and passed the van. Sunny could see another police car approaching from the street ahead of them as residents of the neighborhood stood on their porches, craning their necks to watch the ruckus.

Trying to avoid the inevitable, the maroon car whipped around a corner and crashed into the rear of a garbage truck parked at the curb. A screaming mother yanked her child from his tricycle on the sidewalk and ran in the opposite direction. Three patrol cars, in a chaos of whipping red and blue lights and a cacophony of wailing sirens, converged on the smashed car, which spewed steam from the crumpled hood.

Sunny screeched to a stop at the corner, and Kale, the camera on his shoulder, jumped out and ran toward the cluster of vehicles. Snatching a mike and a battery pack from the back of the van, she strapped the pack around her waist as she ran behind him.

Another patrol car roared to a stop, blocking their path as five officers, guns drawn, spilled from the three other police units and took positions of cover.

"Throw down your weapons," one of the cops called, "and come out with your hands in the air."

For a moment everything was so quiet that the only thing Sunny heard was the hiss of the damaged radiator, the rattle of dried palm fronds, and her own ragged breathing.

First one, then the other door opened slowly. Three men emerged, hands atop their heads. The fourth stumbled out, whining, "Hey, man, I'm hurt. My leg is bleeding."

"Well, well," one of the older cops said, "if it isn't Amos. Got shot up some, did you? You and your friends are in bad trouble again, buddy. Hands on the top of the car."

While the group of robbers was searched and handcuffed, Kale kept filming and asked, "Can you identify these men, officer?"

"Later," the cop said gruffly, scowling at the camera. "Check with the station."

Sunny hurriedly hooked up her mike and stepped forward, smiling. "Sergeant"—she glanced at his name tag—"Murdock, I'm Sunny Larkin, KRIP News. Could I ask you a few questions, please?"

The cop's scowl changed to a grin. "Sunny! Was that you chasing these *hombres*? Hey, I watch you on TV all the time. What's the weather going to be like tomorrow? I promised to take my boy fishing."

"It's going to be perfect fishing weather until about mid-afternoon. I hope you catch a big one." She gave him a dazzling, dimpled smile. "Now, Sergeant Murdock, if I could ask you a few questions . . ."

Kale watched in amazement as Sunny charmed the socks off the seasoned veteran and got a damned good interview. He could hardly blame the cop; Kale probably would have told her everything down to the size of his shorts, if she'd fluttered those long, feathery eyelashes up at him.

When Murdock identified at least two of the robbers as hard-core offenders with long rap sheets, Kale shuddered. The reality of the danger Sunny had been in slammed into his gut. By the time the interview wound down and his adrenaline began to dissipate, he had to struggle to keep the camera steady. He was actually trembling. He hadn't been afraid for himself—hell, he'd dodged bullets dozens of times to get a story—but the thought of this little slip of a girl getting one between her big blue eyes unnerved him.

When the interview was wrapped up and they'd promised to come to the station later with their statements, Kale strode to the van. The sight of the shattered windshield and the wrinkled front bumper shook him even more. It was a wonder she hadn't been badly injured. He stowed the camera and waited, hands on his hips, as she bounded up, grinning and juiced up like some fool on high-grade coke, oblivious to the danger she'd been in. He wanted to throttle her.

"Wasn't that fantastic?" she asked, beaming. "What a story! I could fly!"

She whirled around twice before he grabbed her by the shoulders. "I ought to beat your butt!" he yelled in her face.

Her smile died and her eyes flashed blue sparks. "I'd like to see you try it! What's the matter with you? Did the sun in Bangladesh fry your brains?"

"*My* brains? Hell, at least I've got brains! Don't you realize the danger you put yourself in? Don't you understand that you could have been killed? Do you have some kind of death wish?"

"And I suppose the great Kale Hoaglin has never braved a few tight situations for a story."

"That's different."

She gave a disdainful snort. "Because you're a man?"

"Yes. No. It's not because you're a girl—"

"*Woman.*"

"—woman. It's a matter of experience. Don't *ever* try a damned fool stunt like that again."

"Oh, chill out, Hoaglin." She shook off his hands. "Didn't you hear Sergeant Murdock? We're heroes. And we scooped a story that's going to bring KRIP back to credibility. Maybe that will

soothe Foster's feathers when he sees the van."
She fluttered her hand toward the damaged vehicle.

"Forget the damned van."

She grinned. "Whatever you say, boss. We need
to pick up some more footage at the bank and do
a couple of interviews there. Do you think we
should call the station and have them send someone else to cover the heritage society do?"

As she talked he watched the animated bobble
of her head, the bright sparkle of her eyes, the
enticing movement of her lips. Her skin seemed to
glow. Its texture fascinated him. He ached to
touch it, to feel its softness against the rough pads
of his fingertips.

"Well?" she asked.

"Well, what?"

"What do you want to do?"

What did he want to do? Hell, he wanted to kiss
her until she turned boneless. He wanted to hold
her against him and mold her body against his
and savor every sweet curve. He wanted to bury
his face between her breasts and inhale the smell
of her. He wanted to do things to her that would
shock her bouncy little cheerleader sensibilities
into the next state.

"Boss?"

"Don't call me that," he growled.

"Yes, sir," she snapped with that saucy grin
that seemed to goad him into wanting to kiss her
all the more.

Dammit, he reminded himself, she was just a
kid, a green, fresh-faced kid. The ten years that
separated them were ten years of hard living, a
chasm of ugliness and abhorrent experiences that
had sucked the gentleness from his soul long ago.
He didn't have any business messing with some-

one like her. He almost had the feeling that the heinousness of life that had rubbed off on him over the past several years would defile her if he touched her.

"I suppose," she said, "we could have someone from the station pick up our robbery tape for editing, and we could still make it to the heritage society function in time to catch the tail end of it."

"Rule number one, kid," he said, allowing himself to touch the tip of her nose, "is never, *never* let somebody else edit your big story."

She beamed up at him. "Yes, boss."

Three

On Sunday morning, Sunny, engrossed in the front page of the *Corpus Christi Caller-Times,* sipped her coffee and absently reached for another muffin.

"Wow! Look at this. We made the headlines," she said to Estella and Kale, who were sitting at the breakfast table.

Kale mumbled something into his eggs, and Estella grabbed the paper. "Let me see." As she read the page, her brows lifted and her mouth formed a silent whistle. "'KRIP NEWS TEAM FOILS BANK ROBBERY.' Well, well, well. A color picture and the whole works. Sorry I missed being in on the 'daring high-speed chase.' Did I tell you that I thought your story on the news last night was dynamite?" she asked Sunny.

Sunny beamed, preening at the compliment. "At least three times, but tell me again."

"I wouldn't want you to get the big head."

"Not likely, but it was a super story, wasn't it? I couldn't sleep last night for thinking about it. I grinned all night. But most of the credit goes to

Kale. While we were putting the piece together, he taught me more about writing and editing and dramatic effect than I learned in four years of college. He's brilliant. Kale, did I tell you that you're brilliant?"

He nodded. "You did a good job."

She wiggled in her chair, smiling and still feeling bubbly inside.

Estella looked over the paper at Kale. "Does this mean that KRIP's good-news policy has changed to 'if it bleeds, it leads'?"

Kale laced his fingers over his middle and leaned back in the oak captain's chair. "It means that KRIP will present a solid, balanced broadcast."

"Does that include dumping the tripe from the sports segment and putting some action into it?"

"Yes. Think you can handle it?"

She leaned forward with one arm resting on the table, a fist on her hip, and bobbed her head with exaggerated smugness. "Can Michael Jordan play basketball?" Her mouth curved into a playful smirk. "You bet your bankroll I can handle it. I know more about sports than all those clowns on the other stations put together."

"At least you're confident," Kale said dryly.

"Oh, it's true," Sunny piped up. "Cherry Morris is her father."

Kale's eyebrows lifted. "Cherry Morris, the NBA coach?"

"The very one," Estella said.

"She grew up in a very athletic family," Sunny added. "Her mother won an Olympic gold medal in track, and Estella went to college on a sports scholarship. Her younger brother won some special football award two years ago. What award was that, Estella?"

"The Heisman."

"Morris." Kale wrinkled his forehead. "Morris. Chapman Morris who plays for the Washington Redskins?"

"That's my baby brother."

"I'm impressed."

Estella chuckled. "And as relieved as hell that the tall pregnant lady might know her business after all."

Sunny hopped up and began clearing the table. "Estella, we need to get a move on if we're going to Padre Island." To Kale she said, "We're going shelling. Want to come along?" When he hesitated, she added, "Oh, come with us. How long since you've walked along a Texas beach and did nothing more profound than look for shells? I'll even treat you to a hot dog and a beer." She grinned. "Besides, if you go, we can go in Ravinia's convertible and put the top down."

"Ravinia bought a convertible?" Kale asked. "I suppose that doesn't surprise me, but she's always driven a Cadillac."

Estella and Sunny exchanged looks and laughed. "She didn't change that habit," Estella said. "Wait until you see it."

With a bit more coaxing, he agreed to join them, and everyone went to change into shorts and sneakers.

Instead of her usual ragtag garb for shelling, Sunny opted for a new white cotton shirt and butter-yellow shorts that matched her straw planter's hat, with its saucy chiffon band and streamers. She even applied makeup—telling herself that it was for sun protection and not because Kale was going along.

He obviously hadn't dressed with any special pains, she thought when she met him downstairs.

He wore a pair of faded red madras shorts and a pale pink T-shirt. She did have to admit that the shorts showed off his nicely muscled legs and that the pink shirt complemented his tan and molded a chest that had probably set many hearts palpitating—not hers, of course. She was immune. Kale Hoaglin was only her boss and temporary housemate, she reminded herself. She wasn't interested. He wasn't interested.

But why, she wondered, if she wasn't his type, did his eyes slowly sweep over her as if he were undressing her? She could almost feel the fabric smoldering under his gaze. And why, if she was immune to his rugged good looks and mesmerizing presence, did she feel as if someone had lit a firecracker between her toes every time he looked at her with that intense, sensual scrutiny?

Maybe she was misinterpreting the signals, she thought. Then their eyes met and held. She could almost feel his hands on her, feel his breath on her face, feel— No, this would never do!

She broke eye contact, fidgeted with her hat, and looked over her shoulder to Estella, who was on the stairs, watching them.

"Are you ready?" Sunny asked her friend.

"If you two don't mind," Estella said, "I think I'll beg off." She rubbed her tummy. "Junior here is practicing his punting, and I'd be more comfortable staying home with my feet up and watching the Astros-Braves game on TV."

"Are you ill? I'll stay with you," Sunny said quickly. She was suddenly nervous over the prospect of being alone with Kale.

"Honey, I'm not sick. I'm just pregnant. And I think I'd feel better staying close to a bathroom."

Looking concerned, Kale said, "It's not time . . ."

Estella laughed. "Don't I wish. No, the doctor

told me last Thursday that I have at least another two weeks. You two go on and enjoy the day."

Sunny hesitated. Was Estella playing matchmaker or did she seriously prefer to stay home? She could hardly confront her with Kale present. Shoot! She was making too much of the whole matter. They were simply going to drive to Padre to look for seashells and roast a couple of wienies on a grill. What could happen?

"We'll be home in plenty of time for Lamaze class this evening." Sunny cocked her head, then asked Estella, "Do you remember where I put Ravinia's keys?"

"I saw some keys in the bread box."

She scooted into the kitchen to check and came back empty-handed and feeling disgusted. "Those were mine."

Kale walked over to the suit of armor and from the tip of the lance plucked a set of keys with a red-sequined heart attached. "What about these?"

"Bingo!"

They loaded their picnic supplies into Ravinia's luxurious white Cadillac Allante, put the top down, and, with Kale driving, were soon on their way down South Padre Island Drive.

Even though the sky was slightly overcast, enough to keep the temperature from soaring, Sunny pulled a bottle of sunscreen from her tote bag and began slathering it on exposed skin areas. Kale watched from the corner of his eye, appreciating the perfect curves of her legs, the smoothness of her arms, the suppleness of her fingers as they moved over her body, a body that had haunted him since he'd found her in his shower. With only a slight leap of fancy, he could imagine those slender, supple fingers stroking his skin. Allowing his mind to meander a few steps further, he could envision her in his bed, all warm and soft beneath him, moaning his name. He felt himself stir.

"Want some?"

Startled by her question, he almost said, "Hell, yes." Instead he asked, "What?"

She held up the green plastic bottle. "Sunscreen. Want some?"

"Maybe later." He scowled and squirmed in the seat. *She's not for you, Hoaglin. Get your mind out of the gutter.*

"I really think you should. With all the scientific evidence about skin cancer, everybody should be wearing sunscreen these days."

"I'm driving," he said curtly.

"I can rub it on you."

"*No.*" If she started running her fingers up his thigh he'd probably ram the convertible into the RV ahead of them.

"You don't have to be such a grouch. I'm only concerned with your well-being. At least put some on your face."

"Oh, hell," he said, holding out two fingers. "Squirt some out."

When she complied, he made a couple of swipes across his nose and cheeks. "Satisfied?"

"For now." She smiled and tossed the bottle back into her bag. "When we get to the beach, you can do a better job."

He shook his head and chuckled inwardly. Sunny Larkin was a piece of work. Who would ever know to look at her sweet, guileless face that she had the tenacity of a bulldog?

He switched on the radio and tuned it to an easy-listening station to keep his thoughts occupied. With his left elbow propped on the window opening and the wind ruffling his hair, Kale headed the car over the familiar causeway that crossed the Intracoastal Waterway between Laguna Madre and Corpus Christi Bay. The Allante drove like a dream. It seemed like a lifetime since he'd driven anything except an ancient Jeep or some rusted-out truck with sprung seats.

How long had it been since he'd driven this route in a convertible with a beautiful girl beside him? Ten years? Fifteen? He fondly remembered trips to Padre in the Corvette his aunt Ravinia had given him for high school graduation. Lord, how he'd loved that car.

"You smiled! You actually smiled."

Kale glanced over at Sunny. "I beg your pardon?"

She laughed and clapped her hands. "You smiled. I didn't think you knew how."

Indignant, he grumbled, "Of course I know how. Why would you think I didn't?"

"I've never seen you smile. I've seen a couple of little twitches and wiggles as if you wanted to smile, but I've never seen an honest-to-goodness, lips-turned-up, teeth-showing smile. What were you thinking about?"

"My old Corvette convertible, the pride and joy of my youth. It was black."

"Whatever happened to it?"

"Somebody stole it about two weeks after I moved to New York. Damned near broke my heart. I felt as if I'd lost an old friend."

"Didn't your insurance replace it?"

He shrugged. "Some things are irreplaceable. In any case, having a car in New York wasn't practical, and when I was transferred to Washington, I leased something plain and functional. On the foreign assignments that came later, it was easier to rent a car or use local transportation. In some of the places I've lived, I was lucky to find a donkey cart."

"You're kidding."

He found himself growing relaxed as he drove the white convertible along Park Drive 22, more relaxed than he'd been in he didn't know how long. Before he knew what was happening, Sunny was pulling stories out of him about the various strange conveyances he'd ridden in, from rickshaws and pedicabs in the Orient to camels in Morocco.

"I'd *love* to ride a camel. Didn't you feel like Lawrence of Arabia sailing across the desert?" she exclaimed, waving her arms expansively.

He glanced over at her and smiled. He'd never met anyone quite like her. She bubbled like a fountain of sunshine. He found that he wanted to dip his hands into her vibrancy, and wash himself with her vivacity. Something about her was magical, ethereal yet elemental. And very appealing. She had a zest for life that had disappeared in him long ago—if it had ever been there at all. Everything about her drew him like a warm, crackling fire on a cold night.

"Camels don't sail across the desert. They galump. Besides being uncomfortable as the devil, they're nasty beasts that love to bite and spit. I'd rather ride a horse. Even an elephant is better."

"An elephant! Oh, what fun. Were you in India?"

"No. As I recall, that happened in Dallas. One of my first assignments as a TV reporter there was to cover the circus coming to town. I rode an elephant from the train to the place they were performing. It's a hackneyed slant, although it seemed very clever at the time. Linda Ellerbee once said that every reporter she'd ever talked to has done the elephant walk at some point early in his or her career."

"I suppose my education is sadly lacking. I've done my share of dog shows and ribbon cuttings, but I've never ridden an elephant to the circus."

"Give it time, kid."

"I'm *not* a kid. I've been a reporter for four years."

He held back a chuckle. "That long, huh?"

She lifted her chin and puckered her lips, trying, he assumed, to show her annoyance. She only succeeded in looking cute and kissable. "I know that I don't have as much experience as you do," she said, "but I'm getting there." She focused her attention on the hotels, condominiums, and beach houses sprawled along the northern end of the island. Her pique lasted only a moment, and then she turned back to him, as eager and fresh-faced as ever. "Tell me about your experiences in Iran and Bangladesh. Was it exciting to report on wars and monsoons in such exotic places?"

He grimaced at the montage of memories that flashed through his mind: smells of arms fire and destruction, sights of maimed and bloated bodies, mewling cries of homeless children with distended bellies, the acrid taste of horror and despair. "I hope you never have to find out. I'd rather talk about camels and elephants."

She reached over and touched his arm. His biceps bunched at the contact. Her hand was small and soft and comforting. "Was it bad?" she asked quietly.

"Worse than you can ever imagine. You're better off sticking to the weather and heritage society functions."

"Hoaglin, I'm tougher than I look."

She removed her hand, and he gritted his teeth

to keep from asking her to touch him again. It was a shame that he'd be here for only two weeks. He frowned at the thought. Hell no, it was a good thing he'd be here for only two weeks. Much longer and he'd start going soft and losing his edge. He'd set his course years ago, and there was no place in it for someone like Sunny Larkin, who despite her protests was a kitten in his world of tigers.

They stopped and paid at the park entrance, then both were quiet as the car sped along the flat road of Padre Island National Seashore, the mid-part of the long barrier island unspoiled by development and noted for its birds and beaches. High grassy dunes, white and wind-rippled, hid the waters of the Gulf on their left and Laguna Madre on their right.

"You want to stop at Malaquite?" Kale asked, naming the beach where the visitors' center was located.

Sunny shook her head. "Too crowded. Let's drive as far as we can."

They drove until the road ended at South Beach, then continued a few miles over the packed sand of the Gulf shore, passing rows of trailers and RVs, families on outings, and groups of teenagers cavorting in and around the water. Kale stopped on a deserted stretch where railroad vine and knee-high grass grew over the dunes and shells littered the beach.

"This okay?" he asked. "It's about as far as we can go without getting into the four-wheel-drive area."

"Perfect." She dug into her tote bag and pulled out the sunscreen. She grinned and held it up. "Bet you thought I'd forget. Want me to do you?"

He plucked the bottle from her fingers and muttered, "I'll do it."

While he applied the lotion, Sunny grabbed her yellow straw hat and two plastic bags for shells. She got out of the car and walked to the edge of the beach, watching the waves roll in, listening to the rushing sounds of the water and its subtle changes as it washed the shore, breathing in the fresh, salty air. She closed her eyes and lifted her chin to relish the warmth of the sun and the play of the cooling breeze against her face and neck. She flung out her arms, wanting to hug the wind.

Sensing Kale's presence beside her, she laughed. "Isn't it glorious?"

"Glorious."

She turned to him, and her laughter faded. His gaze wasn't focused on the water. His sunglasses glittered with her reflection. Even though she couldn't see his eyes, she could feel their unfathomable intensity capture her, stroke her. Her breath caught, and a momentary weakness washed over her as if she'd been caught by a wave.

She shook off the feeling, laughed nervously, and thrust a plastic bag in his hands. "This is yours."

"What are we looking for?"

"Good specimens. Anything unusual. I don't really know much about shells. One of my nieces has a passion for them, and I'm collecting enough to fill a treasure chest for her birthday."

"A treasure chestful?" he asked incredulously.

She chuckled. "Only a *small* treasure chest. About so big." With her hands, she measured the size of a shoe box. "The best time to go shelling is after a storm or in winter, but her birthday is only two weeks away. I already have some collected, and if we can't find enough today, I'll fudge and buy the rest."

For about an hour they walked along the beach,

examining and discarding most of what they found.

"I'm about ready for a beer and that hot dog you promised me," Kale said.

Sunny swiped at her damp forehead and fanned her face with her hat. "Me too."

They walked back to where the car was parked and dug a shallow pit in the sand for the grilling fire. While Kale lit briquettes they'd dumped in the hole, Sunny took two beers from the cooler, spread towels in the shade of a dune, and sat cross-legged on one of them.

Kale dropped down beside her and plucked a can from her hand. He popped the top and took a swallow, then rolled the can over his forehead. "Boy, that's good. I've seen the time I'd have paid a hundred bucks for an icy-cold beer."

"On assignment?"

"Lots of places I've been didn't have ice or beer. Most of the time I was damned lucky to have tepid bottled water to drink. At least I didn't get cholera or dysentery."

"Sounds grim."

"Foreign news events don't always develop near a luxury hotel."

Sunny had the strangest urge to smooth the lines on his brow with her thumb and stroke his rumpled hair. Instead she took a sip of beer. "Where are you going when you leave Corpus?"

He shrugged. "It depends on what's happening in two weeks. Could be anywhere." He stretched out sideways on the beach towel and propped his head on his hand. "Tell me about this niece we're collecting shells for."

She smiled, thinking about her. "She's eight, the daughter of my oldest sister, and my namesake."

"You have another *Sunny* in the family?"

"No, my name is really Virginia."

He scanned her face and frowned. "Virginia doesn't suit you. Why are you called Sunny?"

"Because I was such a happy baby. My dad started calling me Little Miss Sunshine, which got shortened to Sunny, and it stuck. I've always been cheerful." She rolled her eyes at him. "Unlike some people I could name."

"We can't all be cheerleaders, Little Miss Sunshine."

"I was never a cheerleader," she informed him.

"Why not? You're a natural for jumping around and shaking pom-poms at the Friday night football games."

"Shows what you know. On Friday nights I was too busy making hot dogs and hamburgers at the local Dairy Queen. With six kids in the family, everybody had to help if we wanted school clothes and food on the table." She jumped up. "Speaking of food, the coals should be ready. I'm starved."

After they'd eaten and had another beer, they expanded their exploration in a direction different from the one they'd tried earlier, walking a mile or more south of the car.

"Oh, look," she squealed, kneeling in the sand. "We've hit pay dirt." She picked up several shells and added them to her bag. They gathered specimens for another half hour, walking farther south in their search.

"How about this one?" Kale held out his hand to show her his find.

"Oh, it's a sand dollar, and it's absolutely perfect. I wish we had time to look for more, but we'd better go back to the car. We've come a long way, and it's going to start raining in a few minutes."

He looked up at the placid sky and frowned. "It's not going to rain."

"Yes, it is. Trust me."

"It's *not* going to rain. I checked with the Weather Service. Let's see if we can find another sand dollar."

"But, Kale—"

He glowered at her.

She shrugged. "If you don't mind getting wet, I certainly won't melt, but I'd hate for the inside of the convertible to get soggy."

"It's *not* going to rain."

"That's not what my ear says," she mumbled, tugging at her left lobe.

"Your *ear*? What does your ear have to do with anything?"

She sighed. "Never mind."

"No, I want to know exactly what in the hell you're—"

A sudden hard gust caught her hat and snatched it from her head. "My hat!" she yelped, making a grab for it.

"I'll get it," Kale yelled, but it sailed past him. He thrust his bag of shells into her hand, ran, and lunged for the tumbling straw, but another gust lifted it and swept it toward the dunes.

They both scuttled up the high sandbank after it. Kale made a flying tackle, but the wind whisked the elusive quarry from his grasp, and he landed on his face. He cursed, spit sand, and shoved himself to his feet.

"There it goes!" Sunny shouted, laughing and tearing up the crest of another dune.

The yellow straw hat seemed alive, playing tag

like a mischievous fairy, waiting for them to catch up, then soaring away as they neared.

They spied the yellow rascal at the top of another dune, caught in a bit of vine with chiffon streamers fluttering in the breeze, teasing and taunting.

"I've got you now," Kale ground out, muttering curses and scrambling up the embankment with Sunny on his heels.

Just as the wind tugged it free, he sprang and pounced on the mocking culprit, trapping it like a loose football. Sunny stumbled over him, lost her balance, and started to fall. He grabbed for her, and they both slipped in the shifting sand and went rolling down the side of the dune in a wild tumble of flailing arms and legs, lost sunglasses, and spilled shells.

When they came to rest, she found herself sprawled atop Kale, thigh to thigh, chest to chest, nose to nose.

"Are you okay?" he asked.

"Fine. You?"

"Intact." He reached and slowly dragged out the straw hat, which was crushed between them. "Your *chapeau,* mademoiselle." He plopped the bedraggled thing on the back of her head.

With its crown smashed, it promptly slid off.

Her lips twitched. "I think it's dead."

Bubbles of mirth caught in her throat and exploded. The corners of his eyes crinkled. One side of his mouth lifted in a lopsided grin. They both broke into gales of laughter.

Shoulders shaking, Sunny buried her forehead in the crook of his neck. His arms went around her, and she could feel the laughter heaving his chest against hers as he held her close, could sense the rumble of the sound against her nose.

She could smell the delicious sun-warmed scent of his skin mingled with the lingering redolence of lotion and spicy after-shave. Without her thinking, the tip of her tongue went out to taste the enticement of his throat.

His laughter stopped. They grew still. His body tensed beneath hers. Then his fingers moved ever so slightly in slow strokes below her shoulder blades.

She lifted her face and looked at him. His eyes glinted with a sensual awareness as potent as a riptide. Her breath caught as the power of it engulfed her. She couldn't think; she couldn't move.

He closed his eyes, clenched his teeth, and took a deep shuddering breath, as if to breathe in her essence or to gain strength from the salty air. His hands moved downward to the swell of her bottom and pressed her against his hardness.

His face looked as if he were fighting a thousand inner devils . . . and losing.

A drop of moisture splattered against his forehead. His eyes flew open. "What was that?"

"I told you it was going to rain."

He spat out a succinct expletive that made her giggle, and they scrambled to their feet. The wind had intensified, the waves were beginning to kick up whitecaps, and an ominous line of dark clouds was moving in rapidly from the Gulf.

He cursed again and grabbed her hand. "Let's make a run for it before it pours."

"But the shells!"

"Forget the shells. I'll buy you a tubful." He dragged her down the dune toward the beach and pulled her behind him as he ran.

After a few hundred yards, she yanked her hand

away and yelled, "Stop! I have to go back for our sunglasses."

"Forget the damned sunglasses." The raindrops had escalated into a blowing drizzle.

"But mine are prescription. You go ahead and put the top up on the car," she said. "You can run faster."

"Dammit, Sunny"—he dragged his fingers through his hair—"you're going to get soaked."

"I told you that I won't melt. I like the rain." Gesturing with her hand for him to go on, she turned and dashed off in the opposite direction.

Muttering curses with every long stride, Kale sprinted toward the Cadillac. Just as he fumbled the keys from his pocket and reached for the door handle, the bottom fell out of the sky, dousing him with buckets of rain. He let out another string of epithets and hurriedly raised the top and rolled up the windows.

He grabbed one of the beach towels and used the dry side to wipe the leather seats and console, then tossed it into the backseat and waited for Sunny.

And waited.

And waited.

Where the hell was she?

He knew he shouldn't have left her alone. What if she was hurt? He uttered another colorful oath, jerked the door open, and stepped out into the driving torrent. Immediately his clothes were plastered to his body by the deluge and water sluiced off his head, obscuring his vision.

The rain slacked off only minimally as he ran back the way he'd come, calling her name over the pounding waves. His imagination went crazy. He could picture her, her leg broken, sobbing and helpless. Perhaps she'd gotten turned around and was wandering lost and alone. Maybe she'd tripped and had been knocked unconscious.

A quarter mile south, he spied her in the distance, meandering toward him as if she didn't have a care in the world.

She'd retrieved that silly yellow hat and was wearing the bedraggled thing on her head—not that it did any good. In the downpour, the water-logged brim had lost its shape, and it flopped down like a limp ruffle over her eyes, with rain coursing from the folds like a gutter spout.

Every few steps she held her arms out and twirled in circles, lifting her face to the rain. What in the hell was she doing? Violent emotions pounded his gut. He was torn between wanting to grab her and hug the daylights out of her and wanting to tear a strip off her with a tongue-lashing she'd never forget.

As she neared, he ground his teeth, then shouted, "Sunny! What in the bloody—" The rest of the words stuck in his throat.

Her face was lit with a smile so dazzling that it almost drove away the summer squall. And her wet shirt stuck to her body like a thin film that was even more revealing than the bunched shower curtain had been. She wasn't wearing a bra. Less than an arm's length away, her nipples, dusky coral and hardened into peaks by the rain, drew his eyes like a magnet and stole any rational thought from his brain.

He was vaguely aware of her words as she said, "Did you get the top up? I found my glasses. Yours too." She held up one of the plastic bags. "And I was able to recover most of the shells." She held up the other bag.

He was still fascinated with her breasts. His

gaze seemed glued to them. Her pert nipples seemed to entreat him to touch them, stroke them.

Of its own volition, his index finger reached out and slowly circled one tightened areola. She looked down at his hand, then up at him. Beneath long lashes clumped with raindrops, her eyes were very large, very blue, and filled with wonderment.

A raging rush of hormones left him breathing rapidly and conjuring up flashes of the beach scene in *From Here to Eternity*. He rubbed his palm over the swell of her breast. She didn't speak; she only watched. Never had anything felt so sweetly erotic to him.

His conscience told him to put his hand in his pocket, the girl in the car, and his libido on hold. His id told his conscience to take a hike. He could no more resist the temptation of her lush lips than a cobra could resist the charmer's flute.

"Tell me to stop," he said thickly.

She looked up at him with those big blue eyes and said, "Why should I do that?" Her lids slowly closed. "It feels wonderful."

"Oh, hell," he groaned, and captured her mouth like a starving man at a banquet.

Her lips were damp and cool, but her tongue was wet and warm. Her breast was soft in his hand.

With his free arm, he lifted her close against him. Her body was so small and delicate that her bones felt as fragile as those of a dove.

With the rain washing over them and desire firing his blood, he felt like a steam boiler about to explode. He wanted to rip off her clothes, lay her on the wet sand, and take her while the surf rolled over them. Never had he wanted a woman so badly in his entire life.

He struggled for control, allowed himself one last lingering taste of her, then pulled away. It was the hardest thing he'd ever done.

He took her arm and strode wordlessly to where the Cadillac was parked and opened the door.

"Get in the car," he said, grinding out the words and balling his fists to keep from taking her in his arms again.

"But, Kale—"

"Get in the bloody car!"

Four

On Thursday, when Sunny and Estella met Kale in the hallway of KRIP, he gave them a barely perceptible nod and strode past without even a polite remark.

"What is *wrong* with that man?" Estella asked as they sat down at the makeup table. "He acts like a tiger with a knot in his tail."

"Beats me," Sunny replied. "He and Foster have been closeted all week, and the only way I know he's in the house is that I hear the shower running in the bathroom. He hasn't said two words to me. Anytime I try to make conversation, he just scowls and growls."

"Did something happen between you two last Sunday? He's been acting peculiar—make that *more* peculiar—since your trip to Padre."

Sunny shrugged and focused her attention on adding extra mascara to her lashes and more blush to her cheeks.

"Come on, fess up. Something must have happened."

"Well, one minute he seemed to be . . . enjoying himself, and the next he did a hundred-and-eighty-degree turn. I think the rain dampened his spirits."

"Define 'enjoying himself.'"

"Well, you know"—she waved the brush in her hand—"enjoying himself."

"Mmmm." Estella gave her a smug smile. "Did the boss make a pass at you?"

"Define 'pass.'"

Estella rolled her eyes. "Pass: touchy, touchy; kissy, kissy; come to my place and I'll show you my etchings."

Sunny ignored her. She brushed her hair and sprayed it with a light mist.

"Well?" Estella prompted.

Sunny heaved a big sigh. "You're not going to let this go, are you?"

"Uh-uh."

"He kissed me."

"Ohhhh, I see. And Little Miss Don't-Bother-Me-I'm-Interested-Only-in-My-Career put him in his place and stomped on his male ego."

"No." Sunny dropped her gaze and riffled the bristles of the hairbrush with her thumb. "*He* ended it. He pushed *me* away and acted like an absolute troll all the way home." The memory squeezed painfully at her throat, and she looked up at her friend. "I guess he was disappointed. I know I'm probably not as sexually sophisticated as the women he's—" She swallowed the tightness in her throat and tossed the brush on the table.

"Aw, honey, there's nothing wrong with you," Estella said, taking Sunny's hands in hers. "Don't let that network-stud image throw you. He's such a cold SOB that he probably wouldn't know what to do with that thing in his pants if it stood up and whistled 'Boogie Woogie Bugle Boy.'"

Sunny stifled a giggle. "Estella!"

"It's the truth. Forget that turkey. In another few days, he'll be outta here. Come on, let's have one of those famous smiles." She stood, flung out her arms, pooched out her belly, and pasted on a wide, theatrical grin. "It's *showtime*."

Sunny couldn't help laughing.

When they walked in the newsroom for last-minute preparations before airtime, Sunny asked, "Where's Hulon?"

The floor director looked disgusted and gestured with his head toward the windows.

"Oh, no, not again," Sunny said. She hurried to the end of the room and stuck her head through the open window. Hulon was outside, huddled in his usual corner of the ledge. "Hulon! What are you doing out there?"

His eyes were squeezed shut and a tissue was pressed to his lips. "I can't take it anymore. I'm going to jump. This time I'm really going to do it."

Sunny's shoulders slumped as she heaved a sigh. "Hold it a minute. We'll talk." She kicked off her shoes, took a deep fortifying breath, and threw one leg over the windowsill.

A strong arm snaked around her waist and dragged her back inside. "What in the hell do you think you're doing?"

Sunny blinked up at Kale Hoaglin, who looked angry enough to chew the mainmast off a schooner. "I'm going out on the ledge to talk to Hulon."

"No," he said, lifting her by the waist and setting her out of the way. "*I'll* talk to our neurotic anchorman." He stuck his head out the window. Sunny crept up behind him and leaned forward to listen. "Hulon, haul your butt in here. Now."

Hulon shook his head. "You don't understand. I'd rather be lying crushed and broken on that parking lot than facing those cameras again. I'm terrified of that little red light. I have nightmares about being devoured by exterminator cameras with laser eyes. I've tried to tell Foster again and again, but he won't listen."

"I'm listening. Give me a few days to come up with a solution."

Hulon laughed sardonically. "I've heard that line before."

"Five minutes till airtime," the floor director called.

Kale raked his fingers through his hair. "You haven't heard it from me. Be in my office at ten o'clock Monday morning."

Hulon looked pensive, but he didn't move.

"We're on the air in less than five minutes. Either get in here now or jump."

"Kale!" Sunny exclaimed, shocked at his callousness.

He turned around, his irritation evident. "Hell, he's not going to jump. I'm sick of the manipulative little bastard's grandstanding. Have you forgotten that his antics almost got you killed?"

"He's very disturbed, Kale."

He raked his fingers through his hair. "I'm disturbed too. Damned disturbed. Will you have dinner with me after the broadcast?"

"Dinner?" she said, surprised at his invitation. "Okay."

With a minute to airtime, Hulon sheepishly slid into his chair behind the desk. Sunny patted his arm. "Everything will work out fine. You'll see."

Sunny and Kale sat in a secluded alcove of a penthouse supper club overlooking the city. They had watched the sun set and enjoyed the growing darkness as the lights twinkled on in the town. Round-globed street lamps along the seawall and strings of bulbs on the barges and restaurants on the T-Heads and L-Heads glistened over the dusky water. The Harbor Bridge became an arch of golden luminaries. The long, curving jetty, which protected the downtown basin, was a serpent of glowing lamplight stretched across the bay.

"It always amazes me how beautiful the city is at night," she said. "Look over there. It's like a fairyland of ethereal crystal ice palaces lit by fireflies."

Kale craned his neck to see. "You mean the refineries? It's the lights on the plants and treatment units reflecting off the silver paint that makes them look like that."

Sunny laughed and shook her head. "Are you always so literal? Where is the poet in your soul?"

"I think it got lost in the mountains of Afghanistan."

"Squint and look again."

He followed her directions and peered to the north. "Ah, yes, I believe you're right. Definitely ice palaces wrapped with strings of Christmas lights. I see them now."

"And the Miradores Del Mar, the Overlooks by the Sea, along the seawall are exquisite at night."

"You mean those Moroccan-looking gazebo things?"

She cocked an eyebrow. "'Gazebo things'?"

"Sorry." He squinted his eyes. "The Miradores are like spun sugar structures atop a wedding cake."

She laughed. "Nice try, but no cigar."

The waiter arrived with their entrees. Dinner was very pleasant, romantic even, with candlelight and fine wine accompanying their scallops and shrimp. They talked of trivial things while they ate, of college days and family, funny experiences, favorite authors and music. Sunny learned that Kale could be a charming conversationalist when he put his mind to it.

He seemed relaxed and looked very handsome with his hair tamed and wearing a tie with a pink dress shirt and navy blazer. The tie, the first she'd seen on Kale, looked suspiciously like the one Foster had worn to the office that day. She smiled into her coffee cup.

"Something funny?" he asked.

She shook her head. "Tell me," she said, replacing her cup in its saucer, "is pink your favorite color?"

He frowned. "I've never thought much about it. I guess I like blue best. Or maybe yellow. Why do you ask?"

"Because all your shirts are pink."

He plucked at his shirtfront. "They used to be white. And my red shorts used to be a brighter shade."

She laughed. "I presume laundry is not your forte."

"I guess not. But at the time, I was in a hurry and water was scarce. Would you like some more wine? A liqueur?"

She shook her head. "One glass is my limit tonight. I still have the ten o'clock weather to do, and I'd hate to be sloshed on the air. But I'll have another cup of coffee."

After Kale signaled the waiter for a refill, she said, "The show has certainly improved since you've been here. But poor Hulon"—she sighed—"what are you going to do about him? He really is terrified of being on camera, you know."

"I'm not sure yet. I have a couple of ideas. But

one thing is clear; I need more than a week for Foster and me to get the station back on track. I may have to ask the network for more time away— another month or so, at least."

Sunny had been stroking the tablecloth with the tip of her finger. At his words, her heart lurched and she glanced up sharply. "That means that you'll be staying at the house longer. Should Estella and I find another—"

He reached across the table and squeezed her hand lightly. "Don't concern yourself about it. We can keep things the way they are for the time being. My plans aren't even definite yet."

Don't be concerned, he'd said. Of course she was concerned. She'd developed a gigantic crush on the man sitting across from her. How comfortable could she be in the same house with him for an extended period?

Although she was almost embarrassed to admit it, more than once she'd found herself fantasizing about him as she'd lain in bed listening to the shower running at odd hours during the night. In her fantasy, he'd step out of the tub, fling open the bathroom door that connected to her room, and pad naked to her side. He'd slip beneath the covers and whisper lovely things in her ear. He'd stroke her body the way he was stroking her hand now, and—

Jerking herself out of her reverie, she quickly pulled her hand from under his and patted her lips with her napkin.

She gave him a bright smile. "We'll worry about that later then. Now I have to get back to the station."

Kale paid the check, and they drove the few blocks to the KRIP lot.

As he was helping her from Ravinia's Cadillac,

she could have sworn he was about to kiss her, but another car pulled into the lot. They walked inside.

"Come into my office for a moment," he said.

He closed the door behind them and took her into his arms. "Do you mind if I kiss you good night?" His mouth was already lowering to hers.

Her breath caught. She lifted her face and her eyelids fluttered shut. "Do you think this is wise?"

"Probably not."

He brushed her lips with his, gently at first. Then the pressure deepened and his tongue eased into her mouth. She turned warm, then chilled, then warm again.

He lifted her so that her feet were off the floor and her face was level with his, then kissed her again. He kissed her as though he were a man who'd spent a week on the Sahara without water and she were an oasis. Her heart beat like rolling thunder, and her toes tingled as if a blue norther were on the way.

There was a knock at the door.

"Kale," Hulon called. "You in there?"

He hissed a curse and let her slide down his body. "I may throw that man out the window myself."

Shortly before Friday night's news show, Kale caught up with Sunny. "Have dinner again with me tonight."

"I'm sorry. I have other plans."

"Change your plans."

Her spine stiffened at his demanding tone. Just because he'd kissed her a couple of times didn't mean she was his property. She hadn't even seen him since the night before in his office. She'd only heard the shower running at some gosh-awful time in the wee hours. Lifting her chin defiantly, she said, "I can't do that. I'm meeting Carlos and he's already made the arrangements."

His eyes narrowed to cold slits. His molars got a good workout before he snapped, "Carlos is married."

Her eyes widened. "So?"

She started to walk away, but he grabbed her arm. "Dammit, Sunny—"

She shook off his hand. "What is wrong with you, Kale Hoaglin? I swear, sometimes you act crazier than Hulon does. I have to get on the set."

In his office, Kale toyed with a pencil as watched the weather report. He had a giant-sized ache in his gut generated by a pint-sized bit of sunshine in a yellow dress. When the news was over, he clicked off the set, leaned his head against the high-backed leather chair, and stared at the ceiling. Visions of Sunny's face played across the acoustical tiles like afterimages.

In one short week, his world had suddenly turned upside down. Because his relationships with women had always been, if not casual, a great deal less than profoundly intense, he wasn't prepared for the strength of feeling Sunny ignited in him. But in the brief time he'd known her, something about her had played mischief with a hidden, vulnerable part of his nature. He'd been emotionally blindsided. He didn't like it. He didn't like it a damned bit.

Now not only did he have the mess at the station to contend with, but also this strange fixation with big blue eyes and a million-kilowatt smile. How had he allowed himself to become so involved with Sunny Larkin so fast?

Not that he was actually involved with Sunny. How could he call a couple of aborted kisses "involved"? But those kisses were from the sweetest lips he'd ever tasted. No, it wasn't involvement; he only wished it were. It was obsession. He was obsessed with her. He must be. What else could explain a thirty-six-year-old man who couldn't fall asleep at night knowing that she was sleeping only a few yards away? He felt like a damned fool, but unbidden fantasies of her kept him so aroused that he felt like an adolescent in the throes of a hormone onslaught.

Since that day at the beach, he'd been fighting the urge to steal into her room and slip into bed with her. He wanted to hold her close and let her radiance thaw the frigid places inside him. He wanted to bask in her essence and bury himself in her warmth. He'd even tried the proverbial cold showers, but every time he walked into the bathroom that separated them, he could smell her scent. And the sight of the shower curtain roused erotic memories of her naked body, all wet and curvy, wrapped in its transparent folds.

He'd worked like a demon, stayed away from the house to avoid her, but it hadn't changed anything. Being with her the night before had only made his dilemma worse. He was angered by his lack of control, but she was in his thoughts constantly. Her image dangled in his mind like a photograph in a gold locket.

If not obsession, what could explain the fury he felt when he thought of her with another man?

The pencil snapped in his hands.

He'd be damned if he'd allow her to go out with Carlos Mondragon!

He shot out of his chair, went upstairs, and stalked toward the newsroom. He met Estella coming down the hall. "Where's Sunny?" he asked.

"Gone," Estella replied, looking vexed.

"Gone where?"

"I imagine she's halfway to El Gallo Rojo by now."

Kale raked his fingers through his hair. "What and where is El Gallo Rojo?"

"Literally translated, The Red Rooster. It's a dive in one of the worst parts of town. Personally, I wouldn't set foot in the place at high noon. She should have her head examined for going there now."

"And you let her go?"

Estella's eyes narrowed. "Why do you think I'm hoarse? I've been trying to talk her out of this madness for two days. But would she listen to me? Hell, no. The only way I could have kept her from going would have been to tie her to a chair, and in my condition, I'm in no shape for wrestling matches."

Kale spat out a succinct expletive and stalked away.

Sunny got out of her red Ford Escort and walked down the street to El Gallo Rojo, where Carlos and his cousin were meeting her. Even though the sun hadn't set, she felt a little spooky and out of her element in this part of town. She knew that drugs were dealt in this area, and the gaudy woman in the tight fuchsia dress who leaned against the pawn-shop wall wasn't waiting for a bus.

Neither were the four young thugs who lounged around the entrance of El Gallo Rojo. Except for slight variations in size and facial features, they could have been clones, with their slicked-back hair and black muscle shirts. Their jeans hung low on their hips, and their upper arms sported gross-looking tattoos of spiders. One of them casually cleaned his fingernails with a knife that looked bigger and sharper than the one her mother used to dismember chickens.

Tiny fingers of trepidation crawled up her spine as their dark, somber eyes followed her approach. Maybe this meeting was a stupid idea. Maybe she would be wise to turn tail, jump in her car, and forget the whole thing.

No! she told herself. She was no lily-livered sissy. She wanted the story. Swallowing the acrid taste of fear, she squared her shoulders, lengthened her stride, and pretended that she had all the confidence in the world.

Prickly beads of perspiration popped out under her bangs as she walked the gauntlet formed by the foursome, her purse clutched to her like a breastplate. Just as she was about to enter, the one with a scraggly black mustache and a bad case of acne blocked the doorway. She could sense his cohorts circling her from behind.

The one braced across the entrance gave her a heavy-lidded perusal and said, "You the lady here to meet Carlos?"

She gave him a tiny smile—or a stretching of her numb lips that she hoped looked like a smile—designed to be cordial without being encouraging. "Yes, I am."

"You the one that does the weather on TV?"

She nodded.

"I've seen you." He looked her up and down. "Nice." He moved aside and gestured with his head. "Carlos is inside."

Once through the doorway, she paused for a few moments to allow her eyes to adjust to the dimness of the hazy room. The smells of Mexican cooking, which ordinarily set her mouth to watering, seemed slightly nauseating now, combined as they were with odors of spilled beer, cigarettes, and other smoky substances she didn't dare speculate on.

A radio was tuned to a Spanish station, and the loud salsa music masked the hum of conversation. Occasionally the click of pool balls or a bark of laughter broke through.

The place certainly could use refurbishing, she thought as she looked around the room, with its dingy walls and scarred floor. Scanning the patrons, she discovered she was the only female in the place except for a middle-aged waitress and one other woman, obviously a sister in trade to the one by the pawnshop, leaning against the bar. Sunny felt as out of place as she ever had in her life.

She noticed several other young men whose black T-shirts and indolent expressions matched those of the crew outside. Two lolled at the bar; five gathered around pool tables in the far corner; another sat at one of a half dozen rickety tables with Carlos.

Carlos! She wanted to fall on him and kiss his friendly, familiar face.

He'd spotted her at about the same time she'd located him, and he rose and waved her over. As she approached, Carlos kicked the foot of the young man at the table, who then pushed himself to his feet halfheartedly.

"Sunny," Carlos said, "this is my cousin Rico. He's agreed to talk to you about the street gangs in Corpus. Much to my aunt Rosa's dismay, he's a honcho in the Tarantulas. He should be studying for college instead of hanging out with a bunch of losers."

"*Las Tarantulas*," Rico amended, giving it the Spanish pronunciation. "We're winners. We're the best."

Carlos rolled his eyes. "Or the worst, depending on your point of view."

Rico's eyes flared and he jumped up. "Hey, man, I don't have to take this s—"

"Watch your mouth." Carlos shoved him back in his chair. "Talk to the lady. I'll be at the bar."

Sunny ordered a cola, took a deep breath, and plunged in. Sullen at first, Rico soon warmed to her as she pandered to his teenaged machismo. She took copious notes and garnered some excellent information for the news special she planned to do on the growing concern about gangs in the city. She'd almost convinced Rico to appear on camera, with his face and voice disguised, when suddenly he looked distracted, then wary.

"You know that *gringo* sitting by Carlos?"

Sunny turned around. Kale sat on a stool facing her, his elbows propped behind him on the bar. His features drawn into a fierce scowl, he lifted his beer bottle in greeting. The greeting wasn't a congenial one. She wiggled her fingers and winked at him, but his expression didn't change. She could almost hear his teeth grinding, and his glower pierced her like a skewer. Carlos sat facing away from her, his head down and his shoulders hunched over his drink.

"I don't like the way he's looking at you," Rico said. "Want me to take care of him?" he asked with all the bravado of youth.

Sunny bit back a smile. While she had no doubt that Kale Hoaglin could handle a kid whose mustache was only peach fuzz, she didn't think he could deal with a dozen adolescent toughs. "He's just my boss. Ignore him." She continued their interview.

"From the way he looks at you, I think he's more than your boss," Rico said, smiling slyly. "And he seems very angry."

She felt herself flush. "He probably doesn't like my being here. He tends to be overprotective."

"It's good for a man to protect his woman."

"I'm *not* his woman."

Rico grinned. "I don't think he knows that. Here he comes."

"Kale." She gave him a perfunctory nod. "What are you doing here?"

"I've come for you." He plucked her pad and pencil from her hands and stuck them in his jacket pocket. "Let's go. This is no place for a lady." He grabbed her elbow and hauled her to her feet.

"But, but—" she sputtered. "I'm in the middle of an interview. Rico—"

Kale kissed her. Hard. Infuriated by his behavior she struggled to evade his mouth, but her efforts were futile against his strength.

He ended the kiss, but still held her tightly. Glancing at Rico, he said, "I'm taking my woman out of here. Any objections?"

Sunny looked to Rico for support, but he seemed to be enjoying the exchange. He laughed and held up his hands. "Not from me, man. I wouldn't let my lady come in this place either."

She could have killed the pair of them! She glanced to the bar, hoping for assistance from Carlos, but he only shrugged and looked sheepish.

Kale snatched up her purse and, despite her

protests, marched her out of El Gallo Rojo. With her taking two steps to his one, he strode down the street to her car. Her high heel caught in a crack, and she shrieked at him to stop. But did he? No. He only yanked her harder, and the heel of her best pair of white shoes snapped off, leaving her to hobble quickly behind him with the uneven gait of a peg-leg pirate.

She sputtered and ranted and steamed and fought the urge to kick him in his Neanderthal shins. But he was made of stone, and she'd probably have broken her toe. He pinned her against her car and dug through her handbag for her keys.

"Kale Hoaglin, I may murder you in your sleep! What was that macho display about? What gives you the right to cause a scene and drag me away from my job as if I were some pea-brain?"

"I'm your boss."

Feeling as suddenly deflated as a slashed tire, she clamped her lips together and blinked several times. "Yes, of course you are, Mr. Hoaglin. Perhaps you weren't aware that I conceived this idea of an in-depth study of street gangs and had it okayed by Hulon Eubanks, the KRIP news director."

"I'm sure Hulon didn't know that you were planning to prance around by yourself in the seediest, most dangerous part of town interviewing hoodlums."

"But I *wasn't* by myself. Carlos was with me."

"Carlos ought to have his butt kicked. Maybe having to look for another job will teach him to have better judgment."

Sunny's eyes widened. "But you can't fire Carlos."

"I already did."

A sour knot formed in her stomach and inched its way up her esophagus. How had she ever thought there might be a warm, lovable side to this . . . this Simon Legree? She fought back the tears that stung her eyes and glared up at the man towering over her.

"If Carlos goes, I go."

"Meaning?"

"Meaning, Mr. Hoaglin, I quit."

Five

"Like hell you do!" Kale stormed. But when Sunny planted her fists on her hips, jutted her chin, and glared up at him, he knew he was in deep stuff.

"Like hell I don't!"

"You have a contract."

"Check your files, buddy. My contract lapsed two months ago. But even if it hadn't, I'd rather go back to frying hamburgers at a fast-food joint than work for a domineering, chauvinistic blockhead like you. In any case, I don't need your job, *Mister* Network Stud. If all I wanted to do was the weather, I have a standing offer from the national cable channel for twice the salary you're paying me." She poked her finger in his chest. "Put that in your pipe and smoke it!"

Sunny snatched her purse from his hand, jerked the car door open, got in, and slammed the door. She sat there for a few moments, then rolled down the window.

"Forget something?" Kale asked.

Her lips were pinched as tight as the drawstring

on a bag of marbles. She held out her hand. "My keys."

He dangled them out of reach. "Forget about quitting, and I'll give them to you."

Fury blazed over her face like a flash fire. "I won't be bribed! Hell will freeze over before I set foot in KRIP again!"

Sunny shoved open the Escort's door, whacking it against him with such force that he stumbled and almost fell on his backside. She scrambled out of the car and started clomping down the street on her broken shoe.

"Where in the hell are you going?" Kale shouted.

She ignored him. He caught up with her and grabbed her arm. "I asked where you're going."

Shaking off his hand, she stuck her nose higher in the air and said, "I'm going to find a taxi, if it's any of your business."

"You're not going to find a taxi around here."

"Then I'll walk home."

"That's telling him, honey," a woman said in a slurred voice. She was part of a small crowd that had gathered in front of a bar to watch them.

"Oh, hell, Sunny." He ran his fingers through his hair and swiped his hand across his face. "It's too far to walk, and you'll break your ankle with your shoe like that."

She took off her ruined heels and shoved them against his chest. Automatically, his hands captured them. "Satisfied now?" she asked.

"I'll give you a ride, little mama," said a man dressed in a flowered satin shirt.

Kale glared at the glassy-eyed pimp, who leaned indolently on a low-riding black Seville with curb feelers and extra chrome.

"No thank you, sir," Sunny said, starting off at a brisk pace toward the bay and downtown.

"Dammit, Sunny, you can have your keys."

She turned and gave him a withering look. "Shall I detail what you can do with the keys?"

"That's telling him, honey," the woman said again.

Kale was torn between wanting to throw her over his shoulder and carry her, kicking and screaming, to the car, and trotting along behind her to see that she wasn't molested. He'd almost decided on using force when a taxi stopped half a block away to deliver passengers. Sunny stuck two fingers in her mouth, let out an ear-piercing whistle, and ran for the cab.

When Kale saw that she was safely inside, he turned and started back to El Gallo Rojo, cursing the whole way.

A few moments later, he slid onto the stool next to Carlos and ordered a triple shot of tequila. "Women!" he muttered.

Carlos glanced at him from his hangdog pose over his beer. "Sunny give you a hard time?"

"Yeah. Sorry about what I said to you earlier. I can't control her either."

"Does this mean I have my job back?"

"Yeah." Kale bit into a lime, licked salt from the back of his hand, downed the tequila, and ordered another. "Have you ever done the weather report?"

Sunny paid the taxi and walked gingerly to the front door in her shredded stockings. Bugs from around the porch light dive-bombed her as she searched in her purse for her keys. Then she remembered. Her house key was on the ring with her car keys.

"Shoot, shoot, shoot, shoot . . . *shoot!*"

She rang the doorbell, hoping that Estella hadn't left for the station yet. She could hear the bongs resonating through the house, which seemed as empty as King Seti's tomb. Since it was already nine-thirty she really hadn't held out much hope, but to be sure, she went around to the back to check the garage. It was empty.

"Rats!"

Trudging to the patio, she tossed her bag on a table and plopped down in a chair to wait. She felt a little guilty about leaving the news team in the lurch—Hulon would probably have a coronary or crawl out on the ledge when she didn't show up—but that was Mr. Big Shot Kale Hoaglin's problem.

Hoisting her feet onto another patio chair, she crossed her arms and stared at the lights reflected off the swimming pool. She didn't need his stupid job. What she'd told Kale was true: She did have a standing offer from the weather channel on cable TV. And she'd had a few feelers from some of the smaller stations in Houston and a major station in Dallas. But most of them wanted her to do the weather. The street-gang story she'd envisioned would have made a great tape to send out to prospective employers, showing that she could do something besides talk about temperatures and storm fronts. Now that idea was shot to smithereens.

She hadn't signed a new contract with KRIP, hoping to take a spot that presented the greatest opportunity for advancement toward her ultimate goal of being a network correspondent—or something bigger. Ravinia had known that and had given her blessing. She'd planned to stay in Corpus until Estella's baby was born and Ed came home, then move on. What was she going to do now?

Certainly she couldn't stay in the same house with the pompous sourpuss who was now her ex-boss. She'd rather have her toes roasted over a burning pit than endure another night under the same roof with him. Still, she had Estella to consider. They could go to a hotel for the night, but Estella would be tired when she got home and needed her rest. She couldn't go dragging a pregnant woman around at all hours.

She slapped a mosquito that was feasting on her neck.

Tomorrow morning, bright and early, she planned to find them an apartment.

She slapped another mosquito on her arm and checked her watch. Darn Kale Hoaglin! She still had a while to wait until Estella got home, and not only was she hot and tired and sticky, but the blasted mosquitoes thought she was the Friday night buffet.

The shimmering coolness of the pool looked extremely inviting. Pity her bathing suit was upstairs.

She slapped another mosquito.

What the heck? she thought, and shot up from her chair. She stripped down to her yellow lace panties and bra, walked to the deep end of the pool, and dived in.

The water felt heavenly.

She swam several lazy laps, then flipped onto her back to float and watch the stars. She'd miss the pool and the privacy she and Estella had enjoyed in Ravinia's house.

"Ravinia," she whispered skyward, "I know you must have loved him, but your nephew is a dweeb."

Something plopped in the water next to her, startling her. Then something landed across her midsection. Alarmed by the thought of frogs or snakes, she squealed and quickly brushed off the foreign object, then frantically splashed herself upright, treading water and trying to locate what had frightened her.

Two long-stemmed red roses floated on the water next to her. Relieved to see flowers instead of creepy-crawlies, she laughed. Another rose hit the water beside her. And another. And another.

She turned to find Kale standing on the apron of the pool, tossing roses from the huge bundle he held.

"What are you *doing?*" she asked.

"Showering you with flowers. Hoping you'll accept my apology." He kept throwing blossoms until the surface of the water was littered with roses. "Is it working?"

"No. Go away."

He only stood there and grinned like a possum. She wanted to throttle him. "That water looks inviting," he said. "I think I'll join you." He kicked off his loafers and unbuckled his belt.

"No!" she shrieked, suddenly remembering her attire. "I'm in my underwear." She herded roses around her, trying to preserve her modesty and stay upright at the same time.

"I noticed. But don't worry, I've seen you in less." He gave her another one of those silly grins and took off his shirt. "A lot less."

Sunny watched, horrified, as he removed his pants and his socks. When he hooked his thumbs in the tiniest pair of navy briefs she'd ever seen, she squeaked, "Don't you *dare!*"

Laughing, he stopped his striptease, then made a running cannonball into the pool. Water and flowers splattered high in the air, then rained back down on her in a deluge. Before she could escape, he cut her off, breaststroking toward her with a rose in his teeth.

He pinned her against the side of the pool and offered her the red bud. "For you, mademoiselle, with my most profound apologies."

"You're acting crazy." She batted the flower away. "This is madness."

"Madness. Definitely. I also apologized to Carlos. Bought him a beer and rehired him. All for you." He snapped off the stem of the rose she'd mangled and stuck it behind his ear.

He grabbed another flower as it floated by and brushed its wet petals under her chin. His eyes glittered with a strange luminescence, and he slowly lowered his mouth to hers.

Wrinkling her nose, she turned her face away. "Kale Hoaglin, you smell like a brewery. Are you slightly inebriated?"

"Only for you, Miss Sunshine." He gave her that sappy grin again.

"Hoaglin, you're drunker than a skunk. Get out of the pool before you drown."

He tried to kiss her once more. She managed to evade his lips, but he contented himself with nibbling the side of her neck and making forays into her ear with his tongue. The sensation almost shot her out of the water. He pressed himself closer against her, rubbing his chest across the flimsy lace covering her breasts.

"Why don't we get rid of this, sweetheart?" His fingers fumbled with the front clasp of her bra.

She slapped his hand away. "Kale! What's gotten into you?"

He gave her a comically lascivious grin and

wiggled his eyebrows. "It's not what's gotten into me, it's what I want to get into you."

She tried to be offended; indeed, she should have been offended, but try as she might to keep a straight face, she burst into giggles. "This is totally out of character for you. How many drinks did you have with Carlos?"

"Two or three. Three or four. I don't know. I lost count. Give me a kiss."

She avoided his mouth again, but he busied himself with running his tongue along her jawline, down her throat, taking little nips as he went. She wanted to say that his mouth and his hands, which seemed to be all over her, didn't affect her, but she would be lying. Even with him half snockered, his moves were incredibly erotic.

Before she realized what was happening, the clasp of her bra popped, and his hand cupped her breast instead of the fabric.

"Oh, babe," he moaned, nibbling her earlobe and rolling her hardened nipple between his fingers. "You set me on fire."

"Kale, this is crazy."

"Hell, yes, it's crazy. I'm crazy. I've been crazy since I first set eyes on you. I haven't had a decent night's sleep. I can't concentrate on my work because all I can think about is you. I want you so damned badly that my teeth ache all the time." He lifted her from the water until her bare chest was level with his mouth. "And every time I shave I see these in the mirror."

He nuzzled his face between her breasts, stroking his cheeks against first one nipple, then the other before he took one pebbled tip into his mouth and suckled.

The unbelievable sensation snatched a gasp from her and bowed her back. A million chill bumps raced over her skin. She grabbed handfuls of his wet hair and bit her lip to keep from crying out. Never had anything felt more seductively splendid.

A tiny voice in her mind whispered that she must stop this wanton behavior with a man she'd vowed never to speak to again. She ignored it, wrapped her legs around his waist, and basked in the worshipful ministrations of his hot mouth and questing fingers.

Somewhere amid the sensual fog, she heard a car door slam, but she ignored that as well.

"Sunny!" Estella called. "Are you all right? I found your clothes on— Oops. Sorry. Forget I interrupted."

Sunny's eyes widened in horror, and the sensual fog disappeared in a flash. "Kale! That was Estella."

"Mmmm." He didn't miss a beat in his attention to her breasts.

"She saw us."

"Mmmm." His hand curved over her bottom, slipping under the elastic of her panties.

"We have to stop this." She yanked his head away and almost laughed at the expression on his face. The rose tucked behind his ear made the situation even funnier, but she dared not laugh. "We have to stop this," she repeated.

"Aw, honey, do we have to? I don't think I can stop. I'm too far gone."

She rolled her eyes. "Use that line on somebody who'll believe it." She pushed against his shoulders. "Now let me go."

He lifted his face to hers. "Just one kiss first."

"No."

"You're a *hard* woman, Sunny, my love." He

gave a snort of laughter. "And I'm a *hard* man. I'm so hard, I think I may die."

She stifled a giggle. "You're not going to die. You probably won't even remember this in the morning."

He lifted her up and sat her on the side of the pool. "Oh, I'll remember, sweetheart." He kissed her knee. "I'll remember everything."

When consciousness pierced Kale's brain, he threaded his fingers through the raw nerve endings growing from his scalp, pressed the heel of his hand against his forehead, and moaned. He raked the thick hunk of moldy bear hide—it was where his tongue used to be—across the roof of his mouth and grimaced. It felt like the leavings of the Shrine Circus after a two-week engagement.

He tried to sit up, but something shattered behind his eyeballs and he flopped back down. He grabbed his head, feeling sure that a homunculus in his skull was performing a frontal lobotomy without an anesthetic. He plucked something from behind his ear and squinted at it. A wilted red rose. He lay there, his hands across his chest in a death pose, the drooping flower clutched in his fingers.

He groaned. She was wrong. He remembered every humiliating detail of the night before. Including the part where Sunny and Estella had helped him up the stairs as he sang "Keep Your Sunny Side Up" at the top of his lungs.

"Oh, gawd."

Had he really done the breaststroke with a rose in his teeth? It had seemed very spontaneous and romantic at the time. He couldn't recall ever having made such a complete jackass of himself.

The mere thought of tequila made him shudder.

Forcing himself out of bed, he stumbled to the shower and stood under the pelting spray for ten minutes on warm, then another five on cold. After he'd made a few swipes with a towel, he knotted it around his waist, leaned against the basin, and stared at himself in the mirror.

His eyes looked like a topographical map of Mars.

He grabbed his shaving cream, but the morning ritual seemed too overwhelming to perform at the moment.

There was a knock on the door. He winced.

"Are you decent?" Sunny called from her room.

"Barely."

"I'm coming in. Okay?"

He hesitated.

The door opened a crack. "I come bearing coffee and aspirin. Are you all right?"

He hesitated again.

"Kale? What are you doing?"

"I'm considering cutting my throat with this razor rather than face you after my asinine behavior when I came home last night. But I think I'm too weak to make a decent job of it."

She laughed and pushed her way in, looking fresh and adorable in a little strapless blue jumpsuit the color of her eyes. She held out two tablets and a mug. He took the aspirin and downed half the steaming coffee in one gulp.

"I don't think your behavior was so bad. For once you seemed really human. And I thought you looked kind of cute with the rose behind your ear."

He groaned. "Don't remind me. I've sworn off tequila permanently. Not even in my next life will a drop pass my lips." He finished off the coffee.

"Want some breakfast?" she asked, all smiling

and perky, but with what seemed a hint of secret amusement at his dilemma.

"Maybe later. First I have to somehow summon the energy to shave."

She lowered the lid on the toilet seat and said, "Sit down . . . I'll shave you."

Hell, she couldn't do any worse of a job than he would. He sat.

She busied herself running water in the basin and lathering his face. Wielding his safety razor in one hand, she stepped between his outspread legs and lifted his chin with one finger. He could smell her perfume. Even in his miserable state, her nearness started to affect his body.

"Have you ever done this for anyone before?" he asked.

"Oh, sure. Lots of times."

The thought of her rendering such an intimate service to another man knotted his stomach. "Who?"

"For my oldest brother when he broke his arm. For my father when he was in the hospital for gall bladder surgery. Trust me. I'm a whiz. Shaving you is a piece of cake. My father uses a straight razor."

She made a swipe down his cheek, then another. He didn't see blood dripping.

"Do this." She tightened her top lip over her teeth. He imitated her actions. Her finger held up the tip of his nose, and she carefully scraped the whiskers from his upper lip. "Now this." She jutted her chin and stretched her lower lip.

He complied. She looked so cute with the tip of her tongue peeping from the corner of her mouth as she concentrated that he wanted to kiss her. He gripped his knees with his hands to keep from touching her. His palms grew moist.

By the time she'd finished, he was aching to take her to his bed and make love to her until sometime next week. He caught the back of her thighs with his hands and looked up at her. "I may have been stewed last night, but I meant what I said. I want you."

She stepped away quickly, averting her eyes and occupying herself with cleaning the razor and tidying the sink. "I don't think that it's a good idea for us to become involved . . . that way." She picked up his empty mug. "Breakfast will be ready when you are."

Kale pushed back his plate. "Thanks. That was great. I may live." He glanced at his watch, noting that it was almost noon. "Aren't you supposed to be on a story this morning?"

"Nope," she said. "I'm unemployed. But I do have to look at a couple of apartments this afternoon."

"Unemployed? Apartments? What in the hell are you talking about?"

"I see you're back to your old self, scowling and growling. Have you forgotten? I quit KRIP, and since—"

"Dammit, Sunny, I thought we had that settled. I squared things with Carlos, and I apologized to you. I practically had to mug a florist to get him to sell me those roses. He planned to use them on a casket spray."

She pressed her lips together to keep from smiling at the memory of him tossing that bunch of roses into the pool. "The flowers were a lovely gesture, and I appreciate the thought, but nothing has changed. I can't work for someone who has no respect for my integrity."

"What do you mean, no respect? If I didn't respect you, I'd have you stripped and lying across this table, with me licking grape jelly from your navel, right now."

"That sounds like sexual harassment to me."

He raked his fingers through his hair. "Oh, hell, Sunny, your job and the way I feel about you are two different issues." He swiped his hand across his face. "Let me make you a proposition."

Cocking her head, she widened her eyes and fluttered her lashes in a caricature of a simpering female. "I think you just did that. It involved grape jelly."

His jaw muscles twitched as though he had a mouthful of jumping beans. "I'm trying to be serious here. Will you at least hear me out, Miss Larkin?"

She gave him a curt nod. "Certainly, Mr. Hoaglin."

"I want you to take over as KRIP's anchor on the Monday-through-Friday news."

Surprised at the offer, she asked, "Why me?"

"Because you're the most qualified person for the position. Hulon is a disaster. He can devote himself full-time to being news director, which he can handle credibly. I can have Roland Cantu, who does the weekend weather, fill in on weeknights until I can arrange something else."

"Would I be allowed to continue my story on street gangs?"

"The anchor position would give you a twenty-five percent raise in salary, and your weekends will be free."

She leaned closer and looked him in the eye. "But would I be allowed to continue my story on street gangs?"

He squirmed slightly. "We can discuss that later."

"I think we should discuss it now."

He rubbed his fingers across his mouth so vigorously that she thought he might take the skin off. "You can, on one condition."

She raised her eyebrows. "And that is?"

"That I go with you."

She considered his proposal for a moment. Even if he had nixed the gang story, she knew that the position offered would be great experience and would look good on her résumé. Being able to continue her investigation was icing on the cake, but the independent streak in her was indignant at his suggestion that he be included. Another part of her was relieved that he'd be around. Not only could she learn from his mentorship, but her next interview was scheduled with a group from the Cut, an area where most of the dives made El Gallo Rojo seem like Maxim's.

"All right. I'll try it for a month or two. But I won't sign a contract."

"Fair enough. And you'll forget about moving?"

"For the moment."

"Good," he said, visibly pleased. "Now, will you have dinner with me tonight?"

"Estella and I were going to a movie."

"I'll take you both to dinner, then we can go to the movie together." He checked his watch. "If you'll excuse me, Foster and I have a tee time at the country club in about an hour. We're courting a couple of potential advertisers."

"I wouldn't count on it."

He wrinkled his brow. "Why not?"

"Scattered thunderstorms in the early afternoon. Being on a golf course when there's lightning is dangerous."

"The paper didn't mention thunderstorms."

She sighed. "The paper is wrong. Trust me."

He looked skeptical. "Your ear again?"

"My ear and a funny little squiggle up my back. After twenty-two years, I've learned to interpret all the signals."

"Twenty-two? I thought you were twenty-six."

"I am. I didn't get struck by lightning until I was four."

He frowned. "Struck by lightning? You want to run that by me again?"

"When I was four years old, my older brother and I were playing outside one summer afternoon. A sudden thunderstorm hit, and we took shelter under a huge oak tree near our barn. A bolt of lightning struck the tree and split it in half. My brother was only dazed, but I was unconscious for five days."

"Are you sure the lightning hit you? Maybe a falling limb knocked you out."

"Nope. The soles on Neil's and my sneakers were melted and the metal snaps on his shirt were fused shut. He still has faint scars on his chest from the burn. They're about the size of a pencil eraser, here, here, and here," she said, pointing a row along her own chest. "My grandmother was the first one to notice that after the incident I could predict the weather. She said it was a gift."

She could tell from his expression that he wasn't buying her story, which was why she usually kept it to herself. She wished that she hadn't told him.

"And I suppose," he said cynically, "that your brother can predict the weather as well?"

"No," she said, clamping her mouth shut and refusing to say more.

He smiled indulgently. "Sweetheart, don't ever

tell the hard cases at the network about your signals and being struck by lightning. They'll think you're nuts." He tossed his napkin on the table and stood.

"You don't believe me, do you? You're still planning to play golf."

He leaned over, kissed her nose, and smiled. "I'll take my chances."

Six

Kale, Foster, and their prospective advertisers sat in the clubhouse and watched it rain. The first roll of thunder had boomed when they were on the green of the fourth hole, and they'd had to run for it.

"She predicted scattered thunderstorms," Kale said to no one in particular.

"Who? Sunny?" Foster asked. When Kale nodded, he said, "Why didn't you tell us?"

"You don't believe that hogwash Sunny spouts, do you?"

"Are you talking about Sunny Larkin, the KRIP weather forecaster?" asked George Withers, one of the foursome. "Fine job she does. Missed her last night. I always watch her on the ten o'clock news. Was she sick?"

"No," Kale said. "She was . . . on another assignment."

"Damned shame," George said. "If she'd been on, we'd have been warned and could have picked another tee time to miss this frog strangler."

"Oh, I don't know," Kale said. "She must have

made a lucky guess. Afternoon thunderstorms are common here this time of year."

"I don't think Sunny has ever been wrong," said Harvey Levine, the other member of their group. "My son got interested in weather forecasting and did a term paper on it last year. As part of his research, he checked Sunny's predictions against the Weather Service's for the whole semester. The majority of the time, Sunny and the service agreed, but when they didn't, she was always right. She's a bright little lady."

"She's taking over Monday night as news anchor," Kale said. Foster's brows rose in surprise but he didn't comment.

"That so? Getting rid of that Eubanks fellow who acts like a goosed rabbit?" George asked.

"He's focusing on other duties behind the camera," Kale told him, trying to keep a straight face.

"Glad to hear that. Glad to hear about Sunny Larkin too. She did a fine job with that story about the bank robbery. Gutsy gal. Think you might have you a winner there. That being the case, I expect I can swing some of my company's advertising budget your way. How about you, Harv?"

"Rats!" Sunny slammed down the receiver. "The phone's on the fritz again. What good is the darned thing if it works only half the time?"

"I reported it for the third time yesterday," Estella said. "They promised to send someone out Monday to check it, but I think they're laying new cable or something. Anyway, that was their excuse for intermittent service."

"I wanted to find out the screening times for the movie, and I can't find the newspaper."

"I think Kale took it with him."

Sunny laughed. "Good. He can read it while he watches the rain at the golf course."

"Didn't you warn him?"

"Sure I warned him. But Mr. Smarty Pants didn't believe me. Sometimes he can be so hard-nosed. I wonder if I've made a mistake accepting the anchor position and agreeing to stay here under the same roof with him." She plopped down on the den sofa next to where Estella sat stretched out in a burgundy leather recliner. "Sometimes I want to pinch his head off, and other times I'm very drawn to him. He's a powerfully sexy man. Being around him is scary."

"Having the anchor spot is a big break for you. And as for the other, why don't you let nature take its course?" Estella grinned. "From what I saw last night, your natures are moving right along."

Sunny felt her face grow pink. She kept her eyes down, picking at a thread in the welting of the flame-stitched couch. "He'd had too much to drink."

"Maybe so, but it seems to me that having a snootful only let down his inhibitions. The man has the hots for you in a bad way, sweetie."

"Oh, I know he has the hots for me. But that's the problem. I don't want to be simply a handy access for his temporary urges. I'm not into recreational sex."

Estella looked at her sharply. "Sunny, are you falling in love with him?"

"I don't know. That would be the pits, wouldn't it? I don't think I've ever really been in love. What does it feel like?"

Estella smiled. "Different ways at different times. But in the beginning, he's on your mind constantly, like an obsession. And there's a sweet ache here." She patted her chest, then grinned. "And another fevered one . . . lower down."

"Sounds like a virus."

"May be." She rubbed her hand across the mound of her pregnancy. "It sure made my belly swell."

Sunny laughed. "I don't think I'm ready for that yet, but I'm afraid I have all the other symptoms. Maybe I need to take a tonic or something, have a good purge, as my grandmother used to say, because falling in love with Kale Hoaglin would be the worst thing I've ever done. Nothing could come of a relationship with him except a bushel of heartache. In another couple of months our paths will be going in different directions, and I'll probably never see him again except on television."

"Oh, honey, love is such a special thing, and it comes along so seldom that you can't toss it aside without giving it a chance. If it's real and grows strong, people have a way of working out logistics. Look at Ed and me. I don't see him for long periods of time, but when I think of the alternative, I wouldn't have it any other way."

"Just listen to us," Sunny said, jumping up. "We sound like something out of 'Dear Abby.' How about a lemonade?"

That evening Sunny and Kale ended up alone again for dinner. Sunny pushed most of her fish around on her plate instead of eating it, which was unusual for her, since she ordinarily had a voracious appetite. Odd, too, since the informal restaurant, a floating barge permanently docked at the T-Head, was one of her favorite places to eat. She squirmed in her chair.

She wished Estella hadn't begged off. Her friend

had used her pregnancy as an excuse again, saying that her stomach preferred a simple cup of yogurt to catfish and that her feet swelled just thinking about sitting for two hours at a movie. Sunny sighed.

"Something wrong?" Kale asked. "You've been very quiet tonight."

"I don't know exactly. I feel restless. Peculiar."

"Weather signals? Should we have brought an umbrella?"

She glanced up at him sharply, searching for some sign of ridicule in his expression but finding instead that his mien was pleasant and open. "No, the only thing unusual in the weather is a tropical depression in the Gulf, but it will go inland near New Orleans without forming into a hurricane."

"Are you sure?"

"Positive. During hurricane season, people around here get very antsy when storms start heading into the Gulf. This one will hit land Tuesday night."

He signed the check and took a last sip of coffee. "How far ahead can you accurately predict the weather?"

"I can be fairly certain about a week before and positive for three days. Does this mean that you're beginning to believe me?"

He smiled. "Let's say I've decided to keep an open mind. Especially since you're the one responsible for Foster and my signing up two big advertising accounts. Until George Withers and Harvey Levine started raving about you this afternoon, I didn't realize that you're such a local celebrity. You're well respected in Corpus."

"Does that surprise you?" she asked, mildly affronted.

"Everything about you surprises me, Sunny. Particularly the way I feel about you."

"Oh?" She widened her eyes, waiting for him to elaborate.

"We'll discuss it later. In detail." He smiled. "Ready?"

They walked outside into the deepening shadows of the balmy evening. The restless feeling Sunny had felt earlier had escalated to an uneasiness that was at variance with the quiet, winding-down mood of their surroundings. Palm trees rustled in the bay breeze; boats were being moored in their slips; thin traffic moved at a lazy pace. A few sea gulls, crying overhead, were making their last passes of the day before settling for the night.

"I'm looking forward to the movie," Kale said, his hand at her back steering her toward the parking lot. "I can't remember when I've seen a film without having to read English subtitles."

He stopped and looked around, a puzzled look on his face. "I could have sworn that this is where we parked the car."

"Me too. Do you suppose it's one row over?"

They searched the entire lot. The white Cadillac Allante was gone.

"Damn!" Kale said, scowling and raking his fingers through his hair. "I can't believe we've been ripped off. Let's go call the cops."

Sunny was as angry and dismayed as Kale was. He'd loved Ravinia's sporty Cadillac, and it infuriated her to think that some lowlife had swiped it while they ate. They hurried back to the restaurant to telephone the police.

A patrol car arrived a few minutes later. The officer, a no-nonsense veteran, took down the information on the car. "A vehicle like this," he said, tapping his notebook with his pencil, "is a big temptation for thieves, but it's also very recognizable. I'll put out a report right away. Maybe we can locate it before any serious damage is done."

While the officer radioed in the description of the car, Kale said, "I suppose we'll have to take a taxi to the movie."

Sunny bit her lip and rubbed her arms. Her uneasiness had blossomed into anxiety. "Something is wrong. Very wrong."

"Hell, yes, something is wrong. Some sleaze just hot-wired the car and helped himself to it."

"No, something else. I'm going to call Estella."

The phone rang. And rang. And rang.

"Estella didn't answer," Sunny told Kale, kneading her fingers together. "Kale, I need to check on her. Now." She felt as if a bucket of agitated bees had been loosed inside her.

Kale hugged her against him. "Honey, calm down. We'll go check on her, but I'm sure she's okay. Maybe she went out to get some pickles and ice cream, or maybe the phone is acting up again."

Sunny shook her head, feeling a sense of urgency. "We have to go home." She tugged on the lapels of his jacket. "Immediately."

When the patrol car let them out at the big house on Ocean Drive, Sunny ran up the walk, then waited impatiently as Kale unlocked the door.

She burst inside, calling Estella. When there was no answer on the lower floor, she took the stairs up to her friend's room two at a time. "Estella!"

When she heard a muffled moan, Sunny threw open the door. Estella lay atop the coverlet, knees drawn up, drenched in sweat. Several sheets and towels were in a heap on the carpet.

"Ohmygod! Kale, call an ambulance!"

Panicked, Sunny ran to the bed, knelt beside her friend, and took her hand. "Hang on, Estella. Kale is calling an ambulance."

"Phone's out again." She clutched Sunny's hand. "No time for . . . ambulance," she gasped. "This baby is . . . coming."

"Oh, no! No! Pant and blow. Blow, blow, blow. Don't push. For God's sake, don't push!"

Kale rushed in. "The phone's not working, and I can't find your damned car keys! Your Escort is blocking Estella's car. I'll run next door and—"

Estella cried out as a contraction heaved her body. Kale blanched.

"There's no time," Sunny said, a calmness flowing over her. She picked up the clean linen from where Estella had obviously dropped it. "Help me get this under her. Blow, Estella, blow!"

"But we can't—"

"The hell we can't!"

"Wait a second." Kale rushed into the adjoining bath, and there was a loud crash before he dashed out, dragging a shower curtain, just as Estella screamed with another contraction. He thrust the plastic at Sunny. "I'll lift her and you fix the bed."

He smiled at Estella and said gently, "Don't worry about a thing, sweetheart. We've got it under control."

Estella tried to laugh, but her sweat-soaked face turned into a grimace as her body bucked.

When the contraction had passed, he said, "Put your arms around my neck. I'm going to lift you just a little bit. That's good. That's good."

Sunny quickly shoved the curtain and a pair of folded sheets under her. "We've got to wash our hands." She sprinted to the bathroom, scrubbed up to her elbows, and doused her hands and a large section of the floor with half a bottle of alcohol.

Kale met her on her way back. "I hope you know what you're doing," he muttered out of the side of his mouth, "because I sure as hell don't."

"We watched a movie in childbirth class."

"Oh, you have a *world* of experience," he said sarcastically. "Don't we need to boil some water?"

Sunny rolled her eyes. "For what? A cup of tea?"

Estella yelled, "It's coming! It's coming!"

"Wait!" Sunny screamed. "Blow! Don't push yet. I'm not ready!" She hurriedly arranged Estella's clothing and was about to drape a sheet over her knees, as she'd seen done in the film, when Estella cried out again.

Sunny's eyes grew large. "It's crowned!"

Kale ran back in, his hands dripping. "Crowned?"

"I can see its head. Kale, when the next contraction comes, hold Estella's shoulders up and help her push."

"It's coming!"

Sunny climbed on the foot of the bed and yelled, "Okay, okay! Here it comes!" A tiny head appeared, and she eased her hand under it. "Oh, it's wonderful, Estella, it's wonderful. Here comes the shoulder. Take a couple of cleansing breaths. Good, good. Now! One more, one more. *Push!* Oh, here it is, here it is. Oh, Estella, it's wonderful. It's a boy! He's perfect. He's *beautiful*."

The wrinkled little face squinched, his lungs filled, and he let out a wail. Estella laughed and fell back to the pillows in exhaustion. Sunny started laughing, tears running down her face.

Kale stared at the tiny, mewling infant, awestruck. A slow smile slid over his face. "That's incredible. You did great, Estella. Just great." He kissed Estella's forehead, then winked at Sunny. "Good job, Dr. Larkin. Excellent, in fact."

High on adrenaline and the magic of the miracle she'd just participated in, Sunny gave a saucy bobble of her head and grinned smugly. "Not half bad, if I do say so myself." She wiped the baby with a soft towel and laid him across Estella's tummy. "Do you have a shoelace handy?" she asked Kale.

"I'm wearing loafers. Why do you need a shoelace?"

"I think we have to tie the cord. I read in a novel once where they used a shoelace."

Estella, breathing raggedly as she stroked her newborn's back, said, "Forget it. You're not . . . using a nasty shoelace . . . on *my* baby."

At that moment the phone rang. Incredulous, Sunny and Kale looked at each other and shook their heads.

It was a salesman trying to hustle aluminum siding.

A few minutes before midnight, Sunny and Kale, arms around each other's waists, stood at the hospital nursery window and watched Ed Jones, Jr., sleep.

"Isn't he wonderful?" she asked, resting her head against Kale. "Seven pounds and three ounces of perfect, beautiful baby. Won't Ed be thrilled when he gets the telegram?"

Kale pulled her closer against him and kissed the top of her head. "It was the most amazing thing I've ever witnessed."

"It terrifies me to think what might have happened if we hadn't come home when we did."

"But we did, and everything turned out fine. You heard her obstetrician say that it's rare for a first baby to come so quickly. And the doctor said that you did all the right things. I'm very proud of you."

Sunny sniffed.

"Are you crying?"

She shook her head and sniffed again.

"Aw, sweetheart." He turned to her and gathered her close.

She clung to him, feeling comforted by his strength, bonded to him by the invisible golden threads of the experience they'd shared. "Let's go home."

With Kale driving the Escort, they pulled into the driveway of the big house facing the bay. Sunny said, "When the ambulance came, I was in such an uproar that I forgot to ask you where you found my keys."

"In the pantry on top of a can of tuna. Why do you leave them in such strange places?"

"I don't know. I usually put them down with the last thing in my hand and swear that I'll remember, but I'm always losing them. Even when I put my keys someplace special so that I won't forget, I do." She yawned as he helped her out of the car.

"Tired?"

"Mmmm. But a good tired." As they walked to the back door, his arm was around her, and her head leaned against his shoulder as if it were the most natural thing in the world. "I'd love to have a glass of wine and a long soak in a bubble bath."

"Need someone to wash your back?"

His question was the perfect opening for her to put a damper on any intimate involvement between them, and its playful tone would allow her to do so without making a big deal of it. But the simple no didn't come. She honestly didn't want to say no. Instead she said, "Are you a good back washer?"

"The best there is. I learned my skills from a pro in the Orient."

She laughed softly. "I'll bet you did."

He kissed her forehead and said, "Use the tub in Ravinia's room. It's bigger. I'll get the wine."

Upstairs, Sunny undressed and put on a short lavender silk robe. By the time she'd walked down the hall to Ravinia's room, her heart was beating wildly. She opened the door cautiously and turned on a Tiffany lamp, feeling a niggling disquiet about entering. But instead of the sense of foreboding she expected, the room seemed alive and welcoming.

The leaded-glass lamp shade cast a muted, multicolored light over the room and illuminated the huge bed, with its intricately carved headboard and gold silk spread. She could almost hear Ravinia's tinkling laughter and her melodious voice saying, "Come in, my dear. Enjoy!"

She smiled and made her way to the bathroom, which was almost as large as her own bedroom. She sat on the edge of the immense sunken tub and sniffed the various decanters of bubble bath until she found an herbal one that suited her. She ran warm water and drizzled in the fragrant liquid. When the tub was filled, she draped her robe across a silk jacquard footstool and stepped down into the deep bath.

As she leaned back, enjoying the luxurious warmth and the scents wafting up from the water, she noticed the hand-painted tiles that lined the alcove. Her eyes grew wide. Sloshing water, she sat up and peered closer, examining the subject matter of the paintings. Her eyes grew wider and her mouth gaped.

"Studying the art collection?"

Kale stood by the tub holding glasses and a wine bottle. A red hibiscus blossom was stuck in his shirt pocket. She felt herself blush from her toes up. Thank goodness she was covered to her shoulders with bubbles.

"Did you know *those* were here?" She inclined her head toward the tiles, where couples cavorted in a variety of settings.

He grinned and nodded. "They've been here for years. Ravinia felt that their acquisition was a tremendous coup for her. 'The quintessence of early Italian erotica,' I believe she said, by a 'truly inspired artisan.' I forget his name."

"He must have been inspired by the *Kamasutra*."

Kale laughed, poured the wine, and handed her a glass. "And what would a delicate young maiden such as yourself know about the *Kamasutra*?"

Sunny smiled over the rim of her glass. "Quite a bit, actually. I studied it thoroughly at the age of thirteen." She chuckled, remembering. "Penny Wilcox swiped a copy from her parents' closet, and five of us spent all night at Mimi Nelson's slumber party poring over every page. But these"—she gestured toward the brazenly explicit scenes— "make that volume look tame."

He smiled. "When Foster and I used to spend summers here, we could hardly wait until Aunt Ravinia left the house. We'd make a mad dash for this place and stare at the tiles in awe. We even took pictures, although the proportions of some of the characters were overwhelming to a fifteen-year-old boy."

Sunny sneaked a peek from the corner of her eye. "They are quite . . . well endowed, aren't they? And extremely . . . agile."

Kale threw back his head and laughed. Then he kicked off his shoes and sat down cross-legged beside the tub. "Sunny, exactly how experienced are you?"

"At what?"

He cocked his brow at her and looked amused.

"Sexually, you mean?" Trying to act blasé, she shrugged. "Well, I'm not a virgin. But," she added, waving her hand toward the erotica on the walls, "I've never done any of *that* stuff." She waited the space of several galloping heartbeats before peering over the wineglass she was clutching in both hands. "Have *you*?"

He only chuckled.

Suddenly she felt like an absolute ninny, a naïve sexual incompetent. Kale was a seasoned man of the world, one used to women with a level of expertise far beyond her own. Her know-how was limited to a couple of unsatisfying encounters and the information she'd picked up in books. She'd always been too busy working and too focused on her career to have much time for men. And darned nervous about health risks.

She was well informed, of course, and certainly didn't consider herself a prude, but from her paltry experiences with lovemaking, she'd always wondered what all the hoopla was about. Now she had a strong hunch that she was about to find out.

He took the hibiscus blossom from his pocket and brushed the red petals along her cheek. Their gazes locked. His pupils had expanded to endless black depths of mysterious allure that beckoned her with a primal urge so potent that she ached.

"Shall we experiment together?" he asked, his voice flowing over her like sensual oils in a harem room.

She swallowed. "Maybe we could start with something simple."

He handed her the hibiscus flower, stood, and reached for the buttons on his shirt.

Seven

Sunny sipped her wine and tried to act nonchalant as he undressed, tried to look everywhere except at him. But like a compass needle drawn to north, her eyes kept veering in his direction. He was tan, taut, and tumescent.

Her breath caught, and she quickly averted her gaze. One thing for sure—he could hold his own with any of the men romping on the tiles.

When he slid in behind her, his legs on either side of hers, she was so startled that her wine sloshed over the rim. "What are you doing?"

"I promised to wash your back."

He picked up a large sponge, dipped it, and squeezed a leisurely streamer of trickles along her shoulders. Then the sponge swept sensuously in slow circles from nape to waist, spawning writhing little ripples up her spine.

Her head dropped back as she savored the strokes.

He nuzzled the side of her neck. "Feel good?" he asked.

"Mmmm."

His tongue flicked the tip of her earlobe, then trailed downward and across the top of her shoulder. "I'd like to bathe you all over like a cat."

"A cat?"

"Mmmm. With my tongue. All over."

The smoldering tone of his words flashed warmth through her body. "Doesn't sound very hygienic."

He chuckled and snaked his free hand around to cup her breast. Her belly contracted and her nipples hardened. He slid the sponge down along the top of her thigh to her knee, then slowly upward along her inner thigh with a maddeningly seductive stroke. As it reached the juncture of her legs, she stiffened.

"Relax," he murmured against her ear.

"Easy for you to say."

"Has it been a long time for you?"

She nodded.

"I'll take care of you."

The sponge continued its erotic intimacy, evoking unbelievable sensations that set her blood racing. At some point, his fingers replaced the sponge, stroking, stroking until she was mindless with sensual awareness.

Her fingers curled around the wineglass, tighter . . . tighter . . . tighter, until she thought it would burst in her hands. When she thought she could stand no more, great spasms of pleasure convulsed her, shattered her senses, and sent her soaring.

As the waves diminished, the glass tipped in her lax hands and wine spilled into the water. She fell back against him, boneless, deliciously sated.

"Relaxed now?" he asked.

"Like an overcooked noodle."

He laughed softly and took the glass from her hand. "Ready for the next experiment?"

Languishing against his chest, she sighed. "Give me an hour or two."

"I can't wait that long, love."

"Oh," she said, realizing her selfishness, "I'm sorry. I forgot that you . . . you . . ."

"Don't concern yourself. We have the rest of the night."

He pulled the plug and set her wineglass aside. When he'd rinsed the bubbles from their bodies, he dried her slowly, stopping to kiss and caress as he completed his task. By the time he'd finished, she was aroused again. And his similar state was obvious.

He swept her into his arms, carried her to his room, and placed her on his bed. She looked at the ceiling and giggled. "I'm not sure I can do this with Farrah Fawcett watching."

"The last vestige of my youth. I'd forgotten it was there." He stood on the bed, ripped the old poster down, then wadded it and threw it in the trash. Stretching out beside her, he kissed her languidly and ran his hands over her body. "It isn't Farrah that I've lain here night after night fantasizing about. She's an also-ran compared to you, and I'd rather have the real thing."

His kisses became more fervid, his tongue an instrument of sweet torture. "Touch me," he said. And when she did, he became a wild man, taking her to heights of longing she didn't know were possible.

At the moment when she couldn't stand the tension a moment longer, he reached for a packet and knelt between her knees to roll on protection.

His gaze, so intense that it heated her skin and robbed her of thought, traveled over her, setting off flash fires as it went. His hands slid up her thighs until his thumbs tangled in her delta of curls. "Never have I felt about a woman as I feel about you. I want to bring you joy, and I want to see it happen."

He entered her slowly and when she was full, he stroked and caressed her, murmuring love words and praises for her body until she caught the thrusting rhythm. Her legs circled his hips, and they joined the primitive dance together. Eyes locked, they grew hot and slick, moving and moaning, savoring and struggling until they were sucked into the raging winds of a cyclone and spiraled into a turbulent climax.

When the last tumultuous pulsation had passed, Kale rolled to one side and pulled her into his arms. "Talk to me, love. How do you feel?"

She signed and snuggled against his damp body. "Like Dorothy just after she discovered the Land of Oz. You must be the wizard."

"No, I'm the tin woodman. I've just found my heart."

The telephone awakened them at eight o'clock the next morning.

"Tell them to go away," Sunny mumbled, covering her head with a pillow.

Kale spoke into the receiver for a few moments, then lifted the pillow and kissed her cheek. "You're not going to sleep the day away, are you?"

Squinting up at him with bleary eyes, she said, "I certainly didn't get any sleep last night. Anyway, I don't think I can move. I'm discovering that you have to be in training for"—she waved her hand feebly, then let it plop back on the bed—"Italian calisthenics."

"How about a nice warm bath?"

She moaned and gave him a you've-got-to-be-kidding look. "That's the way this thing got started."

"Are you really sore, sweetheart?"

"Let's put it this way: I wouldn't want to go horseback riding today."

He pulled the sheet away and kissed her bare bottom. "I'm sorry."

"That's not where I hurt."

He gave her a wicked grin. "I can kiss there too."

"Kale Hoaglin! It's broad daylight!"

He laughed and flipped the sheet back over her. "Okay, okay, my inhibited Miss Sunshine." He kissed her shoulder. "Go back to sleep. I'm going to pick up the Allante."

"Did they find it already?"

"Yes. Not too far from where we had dinner. The officer who called said that some kids probably took it joyriding. At least it's intact. I'm going to make coffee and get dressed. If you're up before I get back, I'll leave a mixture by the bathtub that should help."

"What kind of mixture?" she mumbled, still drowsy.

"A cup of Epsom salts and a cup of baking soda. Soak in it for a few minutes, then allow your body to air-dry. It does wonders."

"You certainly seem to know a lot about such things."

He chuckled. "It's the formula I use for jet lag. I've never tried it for anything else."

Sunny tried to go back to sleep, but the bed smelled of Kale and their lovemaking. Memories of their night together brought the heat of a blush. She didn't understand how he could call her inhibited after the things they'd done. Was there more?

She dozed, roused periodically by sounds from the shower and drawers being opened and closed. True sleep was impossible. Too much buzzed in her head. Her emotions tangled with her common sense until everything was a mishmash.

Sexual involvement, especially of the magnitude she'd shared with Kale, had turned her world upside down. He had awakened something within her that she hadn't been aware of before, and she felt eons older and wiser. The concerns she'd had about a relationship with him before had only increased. Their paths were set in different directions, and she couldn't perceive the possibility of any sort of long-term commitment between them. Or was there a way?

She finally decided to put aside the whole issue and simply enjoy the moment. No matter what happened between them from now on, she knew that she would never be the same again.

A few minutes after Kale left, she dragged herself to the bathroom and tried his remedy. The concoction must have worked, because shortly after she'd dressed and had coffee, she felt great.

"These didn't come from the swimming pool, did they?" Estella asked as Sunny and Kale presented her with a big bouquet of red roses.

Sunny laughed. "I'm afraid those were a lost cause. The pool man fished them out and dumped them. Have you seen young Eddie today?"

Estella grinned from ear to ear. "Sure have. The nurses have brought him in for feedings. Isn't he gorgeous? I can hardly wait to get home with him. That is, if my mother will let me handle him. I talked to my parents this morning, and Mama is anxious to get her hands on her first grandchild. They're driving down tomorrow to take me back to San Antonio with them."

"Oh, Estella," Sunny said, throwing her arms around her friend, "I'm going to miss you so much."

"It's not as if it's forever, roomie. I'm going to be there for only a few weeks, then Ed will be home and I'll be back at work. Besides," Estella said, cutting her eyes to Kale, "I get the feeling that you won't be too lonely in that big house."

Sunny felt her face blaze, and Estella chuckled. Was their new relationship *that* evident? "Still, I'll miss you."

"I'll miss you too. I couldn't ask for a better friend." Estella squeezed her hand. "I want to thank you two again for being there last night. I don't know what would have happened if . . . Would you consider being Eddie's godparents? It seems appropriate."

Touched, Sunny smiled. "I'd be honored, roomie."

"You betcha," Kale said, kissing Estella's cheek.

Estella dabbed at her eyes. "Look at me, I'm turning into a water faucet. Where are you two going this afternoon?"

"To the movie we missed last night, then I have an interview with a pair of Scorpions," Sunny answered.

"*We* have an interview," Kale interjected.

"Scorpions?"

"Members of another gang. Kale insists on going along."

After chatting for a few minutes more, they said their good-byes to Estella and went to the theater to see a comedy-adventure that had been highly touted.

While they waited in line, Sunny noticed several people staring at them—at Kale in particular. She was used to people recognizing her, so she smiled and nodded, but when a very attractive redhead elbowed her equally attractive female companion, rolled her eyes, and made a fluttering gesture against her chest, Sunny bit her lip to keep from grinning. She felt an immense sense of pride. Indeed, he looked very handsome in his usual garb of khaki slacks and oxford-cloth shirt—pink again—with the sleeves rolled up over his tanned and finely muscled forearms. His rugged appeal surrounded him like a palpable aura, and she was as susceptible as the rest of the female population. Maybe more so. She was delighted that he seemed oblivious to everyone but her.

At the snack bar, they ordered soft drinks and a giant bucket of buttered popcorn. Sunny insisted that no movie experience was complete without a box of Junior Mints. Kale laughed and bought two.

Laden with their purchases, they found a quiet corner in the small cinema house, which was one of six in the mall complex. They fed each other popcorn from the bucket and candies from the boxes, teasing with lips and teeth and fingers and tongues. When the last kernel was gone, they held hands, their entwined fingers still slightly buttery, and laughed harder than the other patrons at the funny spots in the film. Laughter sprang easily from Sunny. She'd never felt so vibrantly alive, with her emotions so close to the surface. Everything seemed magnified. And wonderful.

When the final credits rolled, Kale turned to her, smiled, and gave her a quick kiss. "Too bad they don't have balconies anymore," he said against her ear, stopping to circle the inner shell with the tip of his tongue. "We could have gone upstairs and smooched."

She giggled. "With the way you tend to get carried away, the manager probably would have thrown us out."

"*Who* gets carried away? You're the one who makes all those funny little noises."

"Kale!"

He chuckled. "They're delightful, sexy little noises. Why don't we go home and experiment some more?" He splayed his hand across her thigh and his fingers slipped slowly upward. "I'd like to . . ."

The things he whispered in her ear sent a flush of heat racing over her. She almost slid off the seat. When the house lights came on, she was mortified. She grabbed his hand and pushed it away. "Kale! We're in a public place."

"And quite alone."

Sunny looked around, thankful that the theater had emptied. Self-conscious in any case, she stood and brushed at the popcorn remnants clinging to her white cotton slacks. "Have you forgotten that we have an appointment in less than an hour?"

"Ah, yes. The Scorpions. Let's go by the station and pick up some video equipment. In case our young punks agree to be filmed, we'll save the time needed for an extra meeting."

They drove to the port section north of the city where tankers and cargo ships frequently entered the harbor, bound for the refineries or docks along the water. Huge oil storage tanks, grain elevators, and warehouses covered the blocks surrounding the channel. Ordinarily the port was busy with activity, but it being Sunday afternoon a few minutes after five o'clock, the area was virtually deserted.

They turned off Harbor Street and bumped over potholes and railroad tracks until they came to the warehouse region, where she was to meet members of the Scorpions. Noting the state of the ramshackle buildings and the absence of another living soul, Sunny was glad Kale has insisted on coming along to meet with B. J. Johnson and his buddy.

Kale parked the car near the designated place and they got out. "Why did you decide on this area?" he asked.

"Because B.J. wouldn't agree to come to the bar at the Marriott, as you would have preferred," she said sarcastically.

"I don't like it. I don't like it a damned bit. You wait in the car with the doors locked. I'll talk to the punks."

"Honestly, Kale." She rolled her eyes. "You can be such a pain. I can handle myself. After all, it's daylight and we'll be out in the open in a public place. What can happen?"

"Plenty." He scowled and retrieved a bush jacket from the trunk and pulled it on.

"Isn't it warm for a jacket?" Sunny asked.

He shrugged. "I'm used to wearing it on assignments. The pockets are handy for my gear."

He took something from the trunk and quickly slipped it into one of his deep side pockets. Sunny's eyes grew wide. "Was that a . . . *gun*?"

"Yes."

"But, Kale, these are just boys. Posturing adolescents."

"How well do you know these 'boys'?"

"I don't know them all, but B.J. seemed nice enough on the phone. He's the nephew of the next-door neighbor of one of the engineers at the station."

"Sunny, my love, you are incredibly naïve. I'm taking the gun. I don't plan to use it, but I've learned the hard way to be prepared." He slammed the trunk. "I'll leave the video equipment here and come back for it if we need it."

As they walked the short distance to the rendez-vous point, Sunny said, "Something feels funny." She sniffed the air. "Do you smell that?"

Kale sniffed. "Only the usual port smells. Why?"

She shrugged and laughed. "Nothing. Maybe it's just the anticipation of the interview that's making my nose twitch."

He smiled indulgently, hugged her to his side, and tweaked her nose. "Is that like your ear clues you to the weather?"

"Sort of. But it's not just my ears that signal the weather to me. Sometimes it's my toes or my spine. And I get the weirdest feeling right here," she said, splaying her hand across her abdomen, "when a hurricane—"

He stopped and frowned down at her. "Wait a minute. Are you serious about your nose?"

"Sure. It's my nose for news. I thought all good reporters had it. Don't you?" She tried to keep a straight face, but the conspicuous play of emotions on his, from mild consternation to total disbelief, made her giggle.

His face relaxed into a smile. "You're pulling my leg."

"Nope." She briskly rubbed under her nose with the back of her index finger. It was itching like crazy. "Are you sure you don't smell something?"

He cocked an eyebrow at her. "A rat, maybe."

"Oh, look, these must be our guys."

Two teens, big burly fellows with necks thicker than railroad ties, ambled toward them. They wore what seemed to be the uniform: low-riding jeans and red tank tops with a scorpion stenciled across the chest. One wore a radio clipped to his belt and earphones in his ears and snapped his fingers to a beat only he could hear. They both walked with a swagger, their heads, topped by odd-looking haircuts, waggling like the bobble-headed dogs given as carnival prizes.

The one without the earphones looked Sunny up and down. "You be the one on TV. You're ba-aad."

She felt affronted. "Bad?"

"Yeah, ba-aad. That's good."

"Oh, that kind of bad. Thanks. Are you B.J.?"

"That's me." He looked Kale over. "Who's this dude?"

She bit the inside of her lip to keep from laughing. "He's my assistant."

"This is Jeffery. We call him Meathook." B.J. turned to his cohort, who was still snapping his fingers, and whopped a forearm across Jeffery's chest. "Say hello to the lady, Meathook."

He inclined his head briefly. "Do."

"Meathook don't talk much." B.J. said. "And you'll have to pardon him. He ain't much on manners either."

While Kale eyed the pair with his stone-faced intensity, Sunny briefly explained the story she was doing and asked if they would consider doing an interview on camera. "We'll blot out your faces and disguise your voices before it goes on the air."

B.J. took Meathook aside to confer.

Sunny sniffed air again. "Kale, I'm positive that I smell something burning. Over there."

At the precise moment she pointed to a warehouse half a block away, the front windows blew out. Smoke and flames shot out the opening.

Without a word, both Sunny and Kale broke for the car, their reporter's instincts taking over. As soon as the trunk was open, Sunny grabbed the portable cellular phone and punched in the emergency number. Kale hoisted the camera and was running back to the scene as she was still reporting the fire.

She snatched up a mike and waist battery and sprinted after him. When she reached B.J. and Meathook, she thrust the phone at B.J. "Dial the station for me. Five, five, five, thirteen hundred." She shoved the mike and cord at Meathook. "Hold this. Come on, guys."

She took off at a trot, strapping the battery belt as she went. Great black clouds of smoke poured from the warehouse. She could hear the whoosh and roar of flames, feel the searing heat as she neared.

"This is B. J. Johnson here. Hold the phone for the weather lady." B.J. handed her the phone.

"Tina? Sunny. Kale and I are on the scene at a fire in the port area. It's a bad one. Send a mobile unit and crew immediately. Plan on a live report for six." She gave Tina directions, then tossed the phone back to B.J. "Hang on to this." She grabbed the mike from Meathook.

"Can I call my mama on this thing?" B.J. asked.

"Call whoever you want," Sunny shouted over her shoulder. "You guys direct traffic. Try to keep people back out of the way."

Kale was filming as she reached him. "It's spreading fast," he yelled. A series of explosions inside the building blew out other windows and sent long fingers of crackling fire into the air, spawning flashing sparks and acrid, lung-searing black smoke. "God knows what's stored along here. You'd better get back."

"Like hell I will!"

"Sunny, dammit! This place is dangerous. Get out of here!"

"Forget it, Hoaglin. Put that camera on me and keep it steady."

She plugged in her mike and stepped in front of the camera. With wailing sirens in the background and a roaring conflagration belching flames and smoke behind her, she said, "This is Sunny Larkin, KRIP, reporting from the scene of a fire that started just moments ago in this warehouse in the port area. As you can see, there are oil storage tanks only a short distance from the blaze and firemen are on their way at this moment."

They moved aside as trucks and firemen began pouring into the area. Assisted by the mobile crew that arrived a short time later, they continued to film, feeding live coverage to the evening news and following the story until the potentially disastrous fire was finally doused several hours later.

The caustic smell of charred, smoldering rubble and the pungent odor of wet ashes hung heavy in the air as Sunny and Kale trudged back to the car. Both were sweaty and streaked with soot.

"Tired?" Kale asked.

"I'm pooped."

"You did a good job. Thank God we were able to report the fire in time. If the flames had spread unchecked and reached the the oil storage tanks, we could have had a real disaster on our hands."

When they reached the car, B.J. and Meathook were leaning on the fender of the Cadillac.

"Man, that was something, wasn't it?" B.J. asked. "Are we gonna be on TV?"

Sunny laughed. "I think Kale got a shot of you directing the fire trucks."

"Cool." A broad grin split his face. "Man, did you see all them trucks? They were flash. And all them dudes running around with hoses and stuff. They were ba-aad. Me and Meathook decided we might like to be firemen." He elbowed his friend. "Idn't that right, Meathook?"

Meathook only smirked.

After Kale stowed the equipment in the trunk, B.J. handed him the phone. "You still want to interview us?"

"Sure," Sunny said, "but could we make it another time? I'm done in."

"No sweat. Say, I like this TV business. You think maybe me and Meathook could go over to the station sometime and look around?"

"How about one afternoon next week? I'll show you the place, and we can do the interview in a studio."

They set a date, then waved good-bye to the boys and headed home. Sunny was ready to be rid of the grime and stench of the fire, but suddenly she discovered she was famished.

"I need a bath in the worst way," she told Kale, "but I'd sell my soul for a cheeseburger."

He smiled at her. "I think I can locate one for a cheaper price than that. I could manage a couple of big ones and a beer myself. It's almost midnight, and we missed dinner. Popcorn will hold you for only so long."

They found a little hamburger joint still open, and while their meat was grilling, they washed their hands well enough to allow them to handle their food.

When they sat down at the scarred Formica table, Sunny leaned over and said, "Why didn't you tell me I look so awful? I almost frightened myself when I saw my face in the mirror. I look like I've been stoking coal."

"You don't look awful. You look like a hardworking reporter who's just finished doing a hell of a job."

She brightened. "We did do a good job, didn't we? We make a good team."

"A damned good team." He caught her hand across the table. "In more ways than journalistically."

Before she could comment, their food was delivered by a bleary-eyed man wearing a stained apron and whose appearance was only marginally better than those of the derelicts who hung around City Hall. Judging by his state, she wondered about the quality of the food, but when she took the first bite of her juicy cheeseburger, she sighed. "This is ecstasy."

"That's the same thing you said about me in the wee hours of the morning. Is a cheeseburger beating my time?"

She laughed and tossed a french fry at him.

He picked it up and popped it in his mouth.

As they ate, Kale seemed unusually quiet. Perhaps he was simply hungry, but from his distracted expression, she thought it was more than that.

"Is something bothering you?" she asked. "I can almost see wheels turning in your head."

"I've been thinking about the fire. Don't you think it's odd that it started when it did?"

She shrugged. "I suppose all fires have to start sometime. It's lucky we were there."

"Lucky? I don't know. It's too much of a coincidence for me to swallow. Coincidences make me suspicious."

"What are you insinuating?"

"I doubt if it can be proven, but I wouldn't be surprised to discover that those two young thugs set the blaze just to show off and get a rise out of us."

Shocked by his suggestion, she said, "You think they're *arsonists?* Oh, Kale, you're such a cynic. Those boys seemed normal to me—a little full of themselves and feeling their male hormones, but basically okay kids. They might make a little mischief, but I can't imagine them doing something so destructive on a lark."

"A little mischief? Oh, love, you're a real Pollyanna. Don't be suckered in—those kids are hoodlums. Haven't you been paying attention to your own research? Don't you realize what kinds of things gangs are involved in?"

"But they were very polite to me. I'm sure all that stuff is exaggerated. They're just misguided kids. Didn't you ever do something foolish when you were young—like steal a watermelon from a farmer's patch or wrap somebody's house in toilet paper? Don't be such a misanthrope."

Kale smiled down at Sunny, who was curled against him sound asleep, the epitome of innocence. *Stealing watermelons and wrapping houses with toilet paper.* Remembering her words, he shook his head. He'd bet his last dollar that the Scorpions and the Tarantulas were into dope and theft and a dozen other destructive pursuits. With those rose-colored glasses she wore, she didn't have a clue about the real world—which was just as well. He hated to think of life's garbage soiling her, spoiling her sweet compassion and bright optimism.

Maybe he *was* a misanthrope, but he'd learned to distrust human nature through bitter experience. He'd mucked around in the cesspools of the world, encountered things that would shock her sensitive spirit. He would move heaven and earth to keep the innocent sparkle in her eyes, to keep her from having to confront the horror of atrocities and disillusionment that stalked the unsuspecting.

He kissed her soot-streaked nose. "We're home."

Her big blue eyes blinked. "I must have dozed off." She yawned.

"Come on, sweetheart. Let's get you inside. You're exhausted. Want me to carry you?"

She shook her head. "I can walk."

But she was decidedly slow on her feet as he led her upstairs and to the connecting bath between their rooms. It pained him to see her so fatigued. She was such a delicate, precious creature that she deserved to be pampered and coddled and cuddled. Something about her made him want to slay dragons and carry her on a silk pillow, a distinctly new attitude for him.

He started the shower and adjusted the temperature. When he turned back to Sunny, she was leaning against the sink with her hands gathering the bottom of her sweater, a dazed look on her face, as if she'd forgotten what she was doing.

Kale chuckled and began undressing her. When he peeled her slacks and panties to her ankles, he said, "You're going to have to help me some here, love. Step out. There. That's it."

He quickly shed his own soiled clothes and led her into the shower, where he washed her all over and shampooed her hair.

"Mmmm," she murmured as he massaged her scalp. "That feels wonderful. I'd like to do the same for you, but I don't think I can lift my arms. I can't imagine what's wrong with me, but I've run out of steam. I think the beer did it."

"I'm not surprised. You didn't get much sleep last night, and you've had a busy couple of days."

"Not any different from yours."

"I'm used to it, and I don't require much sleep."

As quickly as he could, he washed his own body and hair, then dried Sunny and himself. She stood like a sleepy child as he rubbed the towel briskly over her.

He lifted her into his arms, and when she encircled his neck and snuggled against his shoulder, his heart swelled with such strong emotion that he thought it would burst like an over-filled water balloon.

He slipped her between the covers of his bed and crawled in beside her, drawing her close.

"Kale?"

"Hmmm?"

"I don't have on my nightgown."

"Don't worry about it, love. I'll keep you warm." He kissed her forehead and delicately veined eyelids.

"Kale?"

"Hmmm?"

"I don't think I can . . . you know."

He chuckled. "There's always tomorrow."

"Yes." She sighed and wiggled closer, laying her

head on his shoulder and her small hand on his chest. "I'll make it up to you tomorrow."

His heart almost soared through the ceiling with love for her. He whispered the words, but she was already asleep.

It was just as well. He'd already become more involved with her than he should have. If he had any sense, he'd pack his duffel and head back overseas before things got any more out of hand. He wasn't the right person for someone like Sunny, and he didn't want to see her hurt. Foreign correspondents had lousy track records in relationships. Most of the guys he knew who'd been in the field for any length of time had been divorced two or three times. Wives and lovers soon tired of men who were always off on the next story, of partners who constantly flirted with danger and became jaded by their experiences.

A white picket fence and gingerbread in the oven weren't in the cards for Sunny and him. Coming to Corpus Christi and meeting Sunny was like stumbling onto Brigadoon, an enchanted time and place that came alive for a short time, then disappeared. He'd chosen his path a long time ago. In a few weeks he'd be gone.

Eight

"Hulon, why are we sitting out here this time?" Sunny asked. "I've been anchor for the news for two weeks—and doing a pretty darned good job, if I do say so myself. Not once have you had to appear before a camera, so that can't be the reason."

With a brisk breeze blowing in from the bay, the fourth-floor ledge was a miserable place to be. Her hair whipped every which way, and she had to fight to keep her skirt from billowing up like Mary Poppins's umbrella and sending her flying over rooftops. She would have been enormously irritated with Hulon if he hadn't looked so woebegone.

"You don't know, do you?" Hulon asked.

"Know what?"

"The station has been getting complaints—stacks and stacks of letters and a deluge of phone calls. All about you. The viewers are irate, especially after what happened over the weekend. The switchboard has been jammed today. Even the mayor raised a stink."

Sunny felt the blood drain from her face. "I . . . I thought things had been going well. Everyone has been complimentary."

"No, no, not about your anchoring. Indications are that the ratings are up. You've done a fine job, certainly better than I ever did. Maybe better than any anchor we've had. No, people have been complaining about the weather reports. Complaining vehemently."

Surprised, she said, "This is the first I've heard about it. Roland has been doing pretty well. Of course, the predictions have been off a couple of times, but—"

"Four times in two weeks, including his Friday night forecast for the weekend. As you well know, instead of being fair, as he predicted, it rained all day Saturday and Sunday. Planned family outings were a bust, the golf tournament at the country club was a disaster, and the mayor's daughter locked herself in her room and cried all day because her garden wedding was a washout. Everyone is furious with Roland. They want you back doing the weather."

Hulon looked as if he were about to cry, but he continued. "Viewers felt that you would have warned them, and they could have made contingency plans. I've just come from a meeting with Foster and Kale. Our advertisers are threatening to pull their accounts. The owners have to *do* something."

A terrible sinking feeling flooded Sunny as she realized why Hulon was back on the ledge. What hadn't been said, but what she surmised, was that Kale and Foster were going to restore Hulon to the anchor position and transfer her back to the weather. The whole notion formed a heavy knot of despondency that sat in her stomach like a huge black lump.

Roland Cantu was bound to be disappointed too. He'd been extremely excited about his promotion. And with his degree in meteorology, Roland was much more qualified for the position than Sunny, who merely had a couple of college courses in the subject. She'd taken those only because of a logical curiosity and as an alternative to biology and cutting up frogs.

She felt like joining Hulon in a good cry. Was she, because of this crazy ability that her grandmother had called a gift, going to be chained to weather reports forever?

Despair squeezed her throat. She stared out over the harbor marina, feeling like one of the sailboats tethered there in tight slips, eager to break moorings, fill sails, and run with the wind. But she wasn't the type to run away from difficulties.

Irritation began to shove aside despair. Why hadn't Kale mentioned the problem to her? It wasn't as if she hadn't seen him. Except for the few hours that their work separated them, they'd spent every moment of the last two weeks together. He had helped her film and edit the interviews for the special on gangs. They had laughed together, played together, eaten together, slept together, made love endlessly, and talked about everything under the sun—except the fact that he might jerk the magic carpet out from under her.

Damn his hide!

Just when her career was getting on track, moving in the direction she'd envisioned, he was going to throw up a roadblock. Irritation blossomed into fury.

Well, we'll just see about that, Mister Kale Hoaglin!

Eyes narrowed, lips pursed, steam practically coming out of her ears, she crawled along the ledge to the window. "Get your butt inside, Hulon Eubanks," she called over her shoulder, "and stop being such a wimp. We're not giving up without a fight."

She went downstairs, sailed passed the secretary Foster and Kale shared, and banged on Kale's door so hard that she almost skinned her knuckles. She planned to tell him a thing or two—loudly.

"He's not in," the secretary said. "He and Mr. Dunn just left for a dinner meeting."

"Shoot! I forgot he was speaking at the Rotary Club in Robstown tonight."

Deflated, Sunny went back upstairs to prepare for the six o'clock news. No matter how lousy she felt, she would psych herself up for the camera.

After the broadcast, her disquiet returned and a sense of loneliness almost overwhelmed her. How she missed having Estella to talk to. She was considering calling her friend at her parents' house in San Antonio for a gripe session when Hulon walked up, looking like a whipped dog. He patted her back and said, "Maybe we can find a way to work things out. Why don't you join me for dinner?"

"Isn't your wife expecting you?"

"No, tonight is her ceramics class, and I don't feel like being alone."

"I know the feeling."

Sunny grabbed her purse, and they walked the short distance to the Water Street Market and ate soft-shell crabs at one of the restaurants. She even indulged herself with dessert—a huge brownie, warm and filled with pecans, topped with a big scoop of ice cream. It was better than a second glass of wine and infinitely more comforting.

As she licked the last dollop of ice cream from her spoon, an idea struck her. "Hulon, it just occurred to me that we're not approaching this problem creatively."

"How do you mean?"

"Exactly what are viewers complaining about?"

"About your not doing the weather."

"No," she said, "I mean specifically."

"Specifically, the forecast."

"Right. I think I know how to kill two birds with one stone. Are you game to try something on the ten o'clock news? Kale and Foster aren't around to tell us we can't. And, after all, you *are* the news director."

At ten-twenty-six, Roland Cantu said, "And that's tomorrow's forecast according to the National Weather Service. Let's hear what Sunny says about it. Sunny?"

"Thank you, Roland," she said, smiling into the camera. "Sunny says that I agree with the forecast one hundred percent. But the tropical disturbance building off the west cost of Africa near the Cape Verde Islands could bear watching over the next several days." She did a quick teaser for the last news story, then led into a commercial.

After the break, Sunny launched into the kicker, a brief human-interest story that occupied the last time segment, and then signed off.

Hulon ran over, grinning and clapping his hands. "Beautiful!"

Sunny laughed and leaned back in her chair. "I believe it will work. Roland, what do you think?"

"I like it. I can see it stirring up even more viewer interest when we *don't* agree."

"Right," Hulon said. "We can create a kind of friendly rivalry. The idea has all sorts of possibilities." Hulon bit his lip. "I only hope the owners will agree with us."

"Don't sweat the small stuff," Sunny said. "I'm not without influence."

A few minutes later, as she was gathering her things to go home, the phone on her desk rang. "Hello."

"Is this the weather lady?"

"Rico?"

"I'm not sayin'. You want some action shots of a big slam? Be at the Old Bayview Cemetery at eleven o'clock." *Click.*

"Hello. Hello." She jiggled the hook futilely, then hung up. "Rats!"

She knew from her research that a slam was the term for when gangs confronted each other, often with serious results. Was this a hoax, someone playing a joke, or was it for real? Should she call the police? She hesitated to send the cops on a wild-goose chase.

At least she could check it out. She noted the time and wished Kale was around. Carlos. He lived on the way to the cemetery. She quickly punched in his number.

"Carlos? Sunny. I may have a hot story, and I need you. I'm bringing a van, and I'll pick you up in ten minutes. Can you make it?"

"I'll be waiting at the curb."

She hung up and tried to think. She'd promised Kale that she wouldn't go on any gang interviews without him. Of course this wasn't an interview, but she was sure he wouldn't appreciate the finer points of her argument. He should be back in town any minute, but dammit, he wasn't here now, and this wouldn't wait. She couldn't remember the number of his car phone, so she did the next best thing. She left a message for him on the station's voice mail, then dashed for the door. The phone on her desk rang, but she didn't take time to answer it.

When Sunny didn't answer after the sixth ring, Kale disconnected his call to the station and hit the steering wheel with his fist. "Damn!"

"Problem?" Foster asked.

"I was hoping that I could catch Sunny before she left. I have to break the news to her about switching her back to weather before she finds out from someone else. And call me chicken, but I'd rather do it in a public place. I was going to suggest that we stop by the Lighthouse for a drink."

"You think she's going to be upset?"

Kale laughed wryly. "That's the understatement of the year. She's going to raise holy hell. I've put off discussing the problem with her while we've tried to come up with some other solution, but since we didn't find one, now I have no other choice." He pulled into Foster's driveway and said to his cousin, "I don't suppose I could persuade you to tell her, could I?"

Foster laughed. "Not me. You know how I hate that sort of thing. I break out in hives. Why do you think I put out an SOS for you to come to Corpus and straighten out the KRIP mess? Your type makes a better hatchet man."

Kale groaned. "Thanks, cuz. Thanks a hell of a lot."

When Foster got out of the car, Kale tried phoning home, but there was no answer there either. Where was she? He called for his voice mail messages. The second message was from Sunny—a rushed, garbled bit of information about Carlos and her checking out gang activity at Old Bayview Cemetery on West Broadway at eleven o'clock. An icy finger of fear slithered down his backbone. It was a quarter to eleven, and he was twenty minutes away.

Cursing, he peeled out of Foster's driveway, tires squealing and laying a black line of rubber in their wake.

At five of eleven, Sunny and Carlos, along with their equipment and a cellular phone, crouched in the shadows behind a tall, weathered tombstone with a cherub on top. The cherub's nose was missing and one wing tip was gone.

"Do you see anyone?" Sunny whispered, peering over the cherub's foot into the eerie expanse. The streetlights, which turned Carlos's skin a sickly mauve, made a feeble attempt to push back the darkness, but they only created creepy shadows and dim puddles.

"Not a living soul—pardon the pun. This place is spooky."

Only the traffic from the interstate and the distant sounds of a cat fight interrupted the quiet.

"Do you have the right kind of film in the camera?" she asked.

"I told you that I did the last time you asked. Are you sure we shouldn't call the cops?"

"And tell them what? Have you seen anything to report?"

"If that *was* Rico who called you, playing a prank, I'll have his hide."

Car doors slammed.

Sunny stuck her nose over the edge of the tombstone. "Shhhh. Someone's coming."

She could see about a dozen boys quietly enter the cemetery and congregate about twenty-five yards away. Carlos nudged her and pointed to their right, where another group approached. When she saw the flash of a knife in one hand, she sucked in a gasp and dragged Carlos to the ground.

"We have to call the police," she whispered quietly in his ear.

He put his finger over his lips and shook his head.

A shot rang out, and pandemonium broke loose.

Hunkered behind the tombstone, Sunny tried to call 911, but her fingers were shaking so badly that she kept hitting the wrong buttons. She finally reached the emergency number and explained the situation. The moment she hung up, she could hear the loud screams of sirens approaching.

"That was fast," she said, watching CCPD cars converging from every direction.

With spotlights illuminating the area, police officers waded into the fray, and Carlos started filming. A white Cadillac convertible screeched to a stop, and Kale was out and running toward them.

He grabbed Sunny by the shoulders, and, his eyes wild, scanned her face. "Are you okay?"

"Sure," she said cheerfully. "We're getting some dynamite stuff for the special."

He made an extremely profane and uncomplimentary remark about the special. "I ought to take you home and beat your butt."

Her eyebrows shot up. "You and what army?" She shook off his grip and turned back to the ruckus, which was dying down now that the police had control of the red- and gold-shirted gang members.

"Oh look, Kale," she said, tugging his sleeve. "That looks like Meathook. And I believe that's B.J. who's spread-eagled against the patrol car. Come on, let's get some shots of this."

Sunny sat curled up on the couch with her fingers cupping a snifter of brandy. Kale, glowering as ferociously as a Saturday night wrestler, sat on the edge of a chair across from her, holding an empty glass that had contained a double shot of Scotch only moments before.

"Whatever possessed you to pull a dumb stunt like that?" he growled. "If I hadn't called the police, you'd have been in a hell of a mess."

"Ohhhh, that's why they were so quick," she said. "You needn't have been concerned. I'd just called them myself. Kale, you're such a worrywart. You're going to have to get it through your head that I am a very bright and capable woman. I can take care of myself."

"Like hell you can!"

"Oh, stop making those bear noises," she said, dismissing his roaring with a wave of her hand. "We really did get some fantastic film for the special. I wonder who called me? I could have sworn it was Rico, but his gang wasn't involved. Carlos sure was relieved."

Kale shook his head and looked at her as if she were a simpleton. "You don't get it, do you, Miss Sunshine?"

"Get what?"

"Of course it was Rico. He wouldn't have

squealed on his own gang, but he knew you'd call the cops on his rivals."

"Why, that sly little devil."

He looked exasperated. "I don't know what I'm going to do with you. You march blindly into trouble like a lemming over a cliff."

She smiled smugly. "Reporter's instinct."

He made a rude comment. "Finished with your brandy?"

"Why?"

"I just thought of something I can do with you." His smile turned licentious. "All night."

"Don't you have something to tell me first?"

He looked puzzled. "About what?"

"Oh," she said innocently, pausing to pick a piece of lint from her skirt, rolling it between her fingers, then depositing it in an ashtray, "something about complaints to the station about the weather. Some minor detail like breaking my heart by moving me out of the anchor position."

He paled. "Oh, my God, I'd forgotten about that."

"Forgotten about it?" Her eyes widened. She fluttered her lashes dramatically, relishing watching him squirm for a change. "Forgotten about destroying my dream, bursting my balloon, raining on my parade? *Forgotten* about it?"

He raked his fingers through his hair. "Honey, I meant to explain—"

"And when, pray tell," she asked in a syrupy-sweet tone, "were you going to explain that you were planning to put my head on the chopping block? While you were nibbling my belly button or after we made love?" She affected a wounded-maiden pose and milked the moment for all it was worth.

"Aw hell, Sunny, I . . ." He looked at her helplessly.

"Why, Ah do believe, Mistah Hoaglin, that foah once in yoah life, yoah at a loss foah words. Ah'll just sit heah as quiet as a li'l ole mouse until you think of some."

"Dammit, Sunny—"

"Mistah Hoaglin! Yoah vocabulary seems seriously limited to profanity. Ah'm shocked." If she'd had a fan, she would have fluttered it furiously. "Ah would think that a renowned correspondent with the *network* would have a better command of the language."

His eyes narrowed. "What's going on here? Why aren't you in my face yelling?"

"Me? Yell?" She splayed her hand across her chest and tried to appear affronted. "Why, Mistah Hoaglin, Ah never yell."

"Like hell you don't. And what's with the simpering Southern belle business? What are you up to?"

"I'm sure I don't know what you're talking about." She put her snifter down and stood. "I think I'll go for a swim." She unbuckled her belt and let it drop. On her way to the pool, she left a trail of clothes behind her. From the hopping and thumping noises she suspected that Kale was imitating her actions.

By the time she'd reached the apron of the pool, she was nude. Kale, still wearing one sock and trying to unzip his pants, caught up with her.

"Are you going to tell me what's going on?" he asked. "I've sweated bullets trying to avoid switching you back to doing the weather. It's been frustrating as hell. I figured that you would give me a hard time."

She smiled. "Oh, I plan to give you a hard time." She touched him intimately.

"I'm all for that, love," he said, reaching for her, his lips already descending.

"You jerk!" She shoved him in the pool.

Laughing at the shocked look on his face, she dived in and swam underwater to the far side. When she came up for air, Kale's head popped up beside her.

"What was that all about?"

"Why didn't you tell me about all the complaints the station had received about the weather report? Why didn't you tell me there was a problem? It's not as if we haven't been together eighteen or twenty hours a day every day for the past two weeks."

"Sweetheart, I didn't want to upset you."

"*Upset* me?" She rolled her eyes and looked heavenward. "Kale Hoaglin, are you ever going to learn to stop underestimating me?" She put both hands on his head and shoved him underwater, putting her whole weight behind her action, then took off with a fast crawl to the ladder.

He grabbed her ankle while her foot was on the first rung. "Dammit, Sunny, come back here. You're acting crazy. Are you mad at me?"

"What*ever* gave you that idea?"

He trapped her against the ladder. "Honey, let's talk."

"So *now* you want to talk."

"Love, if there was any other way to straighten things out so that you wouldn't have been disappointed, I would have done it. Don't you know that? You're a victim of your own popularity. There is simply no other solution."

"Oh, but there is." She told him about the experiment that she and Roland had tried on the ten o'clock news.

She kept her fingers crossed while he seemed to mull over the concept. Finally he nodded. "Creative idea. I think it'll work. This way everybody will be happy."

"Of course. If you'd only explained the situation to me a week ago, you could have saved everyone a lot of grief. You don't trust me, do you?"

"It's not that I don't trust you." He rubbed his cheek against hers. "It's that I love you so damned much that I want to shield you from unpleasantness."

Her heart flew to her throat. Of the words he'd said, only "I love you" had registered. She drew back and looked at him, blinking rapidly to keep tears from forming. "You love me?"

"Sure I love you. Why else do you think I'd keep making a damned fool of myself?"

"I just thought it came naturally."

He laughed and kissed her. Her arms tightened around his neck and her tongue met the warmth of his. As always, his smoldering kisses, the aura of his nearness charged her blood, made her want to lose herself in him.

She arched her back and rubbed her breasts against his chest, loving the feel of bare skin and gently lapping water.

"God, you feel good," he said.

"My thoughts exactly."

He kissed her nose, her chin, her ear. "We're going to have to move to the shallow end," he murmured. "I can't do what I want to and hold on to this ladder. If I let go, we'll drown."

She laughed. "And you'd better take off your pants."

He nipped her earlobe. "That too."

Just before dawn, Sunny awakened. For a moment she lay still in the warm solace of Kale's arms, listening to him breathe, registering the subtle male scent that was his alone, feeling his steady heartbeat beneath her hand. After so few hours in bed, she should have snuggled back down in her comfortable nest and gone to sleep again.

But sleep eluded her.

Moving slowly and trying not to disturb Kale, she slipped from the bed, walked through the connecting bath, and picked up a robe in her bedroom.

When the robe was belted, she drew back the curtains of the front window and looked out over the bay. The first rays of the rising sun painted the wave tips gold as they rippled toward the bulkhead across Ocean Drive. It was an exquisite site, a placid scene, reminding her of the surety and continuity of life. Ordinarily, watching the sun rise and the waves roll in exhilarated her as she captured the rejuvenating spirit. But now she felt only a vague sadness.

Her feeling was stupid, she told herself. Kale loved her. And even though she hadn't returned his words, she loved him. She should be deliriously happy.

Then why did she feel melancholy?

And the swirl in her solar plexus, was it a weather signal or was it a building anxiety about the future? Or both? She'd blithely vowed that she wasn't going to worry about the reality that her and Kale's paths must diverge. But that was before.

Kale woke with a start and felt for Sunny. When he found her missing, a momentary panic flashed over him. He'd grown so accustomed to having her beside him that he felt as if a part of him were missing. He threw off the covers and went to look for her.

The tension in his body ebbed when he spotted her standing by her bedroom window. He went to her, put his arms around her waist, and laid his cheek against her temple. "Why are you up so early?"

"Just watching the sunrise and thinking."

"About anything profound?"

"About storms brewing. About you. And me. And what's to become of us."

Kale knew that he shouldn't have told her that he loved her, but the words had simply slipped out of his mouth, and he couldn't take them back. Besides, dammit, he *did* love her. The thought of leaving her was like a stake in his heart.

"What do you want to become of us?" he asked.

"I don't know." She stroked his arm and sighed. "I wish sometimes that you weren't leaving in a few weeks for Timbuktu or wherever."

"Honey, it's my job."

"I understand. And I realize that we're going in two different directions. But still, I'll miss you."

A gut-wrenching pain grabbed him, and his arms tightened around her. "It's not as if I'll never see you again. I have leave between assignments, and—"

She turned and put her fingers to his lips. "Let's not think about the future and storms. Let's enjoy the moment." She smiled, but the smile didn't quite match her usual one. Her dimples deepened, but her eyes didn't flash with their normal sparkle. "We still have several of Ravinia's tiles yet to try as part of my education," she said, laughing.

Her laughter seemed forced, bittersweet. He

ached to lighten her mood and boost his own spirits, but he couldn't think of a damned thing to do or say.

Finally he kissed her and lifted her into his arms. "How 'bout we try something on the third row from the bottom?"

Nine

"Thank you, Roland." She smiled into Camera One. "Sunny says that I agree with your forecast of beautiful weather for the weekend. A little windy, but great for sailing and kite flying. I would caution that we should keep an eye on tropical storm Chloe that Roland has been tracking for you for the past several days. I have a feeling that Chloe is no gentle lady. She started as a disturbance off Cape Verde, but look for her to intensify into a hurricane after she moves into the Caribbean on Sunday."

After a commercial break and the final news story of the Friday evening broadcast, the team signed off.

When the floor director signaled that they were off the air, Sunny glanced over to see Kale standing out of camera range at the edge of the set. His brows were drawn together in what she had come to call his "semi-scowl." She got up and walked over to him.

"Something wrong?" she asked.

"Were you serious about that hurricane business?"

"Of course I was serious. I wouldn't joke about something like that."

He looked as if he were about to say something, then hesitated.

"Something bothering you?"

"No, no, I was only trying to figure out where we could go for dinner tonight. What sounds good?"

"Maybe we could send out for pizza. I'd like to take a final look at the tape for the special."

He smiled. "Sweetheart, given how hard we've worked on it, that tape is as slick as it's ever going to get. Relax. You're as nervous as a stage mother at her child's first recital. Let's walk over to the Lighthouse for some oysters."

She cocked an eyebrow. "You know what they say about oysters, don't you?"

He chuckled and took her hand. "Yep, and I've got to keep up my strength."

A few minutes later, they crossed the wide boulevard that was Shoreline Drive and walked down the T-Head that extended out into the bay. The Lighthouse, a restaurant that sat at the end of the T, was one of her favorite places. The view from the upstairs dining room, with its circular wall of glass windows and doors, allowed them to watch the boats breezing past, their billowed sails as colorful as tropical parrots.

They were seated in a quiet area, and Kale ordered a dozen raw oysters. Sunny wrinkled her nose and ordered a shrimp cocktail. "I don't see how you can eat those slimy things," she said.

"It's one of the sacrifices I make for love."

She laughed. "Baloney. Your virility doesn't need a boost."

"Keep you worn out, do I?" When she didn't

answer, he lifted her chin with his finger. "Are you blushing?"

"Certainly not." She busied herself spreading her napkin on her lap. "Do you really think the gang special is good?"

"I think it's excellent. And as much as I hate to admit it, the footage on the cemetery fight and the shots of the arrests were the perfect climax. I predict that after it airs Monday night, you'll be the toast of the town."

"Aren't you laying it on a little thick?"

"It's good, honey," he said. "Really good. You've interviewed school officials, a developmental psychologist, a sociologist, and a member of the police department's task force on gangs, as well as the kids themselves. You've presented a well-balanced program explaining that these kids band together out of a need for belonging, a normal behavior except that they choose a destructive method to fulfill their needs. You've shown the negative consequences of their behavior and have made a provocative statement. I wouldn't be surprised if you won a community-affairs award with it."

"Mostly thanks to you. Besides all the story help and editing tips, you're a superb cameraman. How did you learn to be so good at filming?"

"Basically from Pete Fisher here in Corpus. He was the best there was. When I spent summers here as a teenager, I trailed after him and nearly drove him crazy with my questions, but I learned. And in some of the field assignments I've had overseas, I often had to be both cameraman and reporter."

"Have you missed being on the other side of the camera?"

"Missed it?" He looked pensive for a moment.

"You know, I haven't. And that surprises me. I suppose I've been too busy with other things to miss it."

A waiter brought their food, and their conversation turned to other matters.

After dinner, they walked along the seawall, avoiding roller skaters and pausing to explore one of the thick-walled octagonal Miradores—or the "white gazebo thing," as Kale called it.

"We'd better enjoy the relative quiet while we can," she said. "The weekend after this is when the big festival is scheduled. Tourists will be so thick around here that you won't be able to stir them with a stick."

"A big deal, huh?"

"Very. Tents will be all along Bayfront Plaza by the museums, selling arts and crafts and everything under the sun. There will be music and dancing and magic shows and plays, booths selling beer and cold drinks and every kind of food you can imagine. During the days there'll be a regatta and an 'Anything That Will Float but a Boat' race—that's always a hoot—and at night there are splendid fireworks."

"Sounds like fun."

"It is. Will you buy me cotton candy at the festival?"

"Sure. I'll even throw in a hot dog and some beer."

Sunny leaned against the pink marble atop the balustrade and gazed out over the water. "I love Corpus," she said, holding her face to the breeze. "Some people call it the Texas Riviera. Have you ever been there? To the real Riviera, I mean."

He nodded.

"I've never been much of anywhere exotic. Was it beautiful?"

"It was okay, I guess."

"Do they really have nude beaches?"

"I never noticed."

"Liar." She laughed. "Where's the most beautiful place you've ever been?"

"Right here. Right now. With you." He rubbed the back of his index finger along the curve of her cheek.

She turned her head and nipped his finger playfully. "Well said. But I mean a place besides here. Another country."

He rested his forearms next to hers on the railing. "Oh, I don't know. Scotland in the summer, maybe. Or Greece. I suppose Greece is my favorite place in Europe. I think you'd like it. Maybe we can go there sometime."

"Oh, sure." A lump rose in her throat, but she swallowed it down and laughed to cover the sorrowful emotion welling up inside her. "Look! Windsurfers." She pointed to a distant pair riding the surface of the water. "In many ways, I'll hate to leave Corpus Christi and the bay area."

She felt his arm tense. "Where are you going?" he asked sharply.

"Nowhere immediately, but I hope it won't be too long until I find a spot in a more visible market. Eventually I'd like to go to Washington. I've always been fascinated by national politics. I graduated magna cum laude with a double major in communications and political science. I'm not simply a Twinkie, you know."

"A Twinkie? You mean one of those bubbleheads who reads the news and smiles a lot to cover her incompetence?"

"Right."

"I never thought you were."

She looked askance at him. "Your nose is growing." He had the good manners to look sheepish. She laughed and hooked her arm in his. "Come on, Pinocchio, I have to get back to work."

When they reached the door of the Parrish Building, Kale asked, "What would you like to do this weekend? I think I could talk Foster into loaning us his sailboat if you're interested."

She thought for a moment. "That might be nice for Sunday, but do you know what I'd like to do tomorrow? Go kite flying. I haven't done that in years, and it looks like such fun. Maybe we could rent a four-wheel drive and go way down Padre Island."

"Your wish is my command." He gave her a brief kiss. "I'll see you at home at ten-thirty-five. I'll have your slippers and a martini waiting."

"But I hate martinis."

He waggled his hand. "A brandy, then. Whatever."

He kissed her again. It was meant to be a quick kiss, but she could feel his lips change beneath hers. His mouth became hungry, urgent, almost desperate. When he finally released her, there was an odd, troubled look in his eyes.

As Kale drove down Shoreline Drive until it turned to Ocean Drive, parts of his conversation with Sunny replayed in his head, troubling him, seriously troubling him. He'd never really loved anyone before, not the deep kind of love he felt for Sunny. And he'd been so wrapped up in loving her, delighting in her, that he'd refused to think about the future. Now it was time for him to get his head out of the sand and consider the situation because, for damn sure, he intended for them to be together. He wasn't about to let her go tooling off into the sunset by herself. Who would look after her?

He loved her. She'd brought sunshine back into his life, filled a dark hole he hadn't even realized was there. He couldn't imagine returning to some godforsaken spot on the globe alone. The thought of being without her sent cold chills over him.

Parking in the driveway, he walked around to the swimming pool and stared at the water. He could almost hear her laughter lilting across the blue expanse.

He'd think of something. He had to.

His was black with a red-eyed golden dragon and a long black tail; hers was yellow with a happy-faced orange sun and a yellow streamer.

"Mine is better than yours," Sunny shrieked.

"That sissy thing? It is not."

"It is too. It's a hundred feet higher."

"A hundred feet?" Kale gave her an oblique glance. "You have a serious distance-perception problem." He let out the string on his kite, and it soared higher, well beyond Sunny's. "How about them apples, Miss Smarty-Pants?"

"That's not fair. You're bigger than I am."

Kale laughed. "What does that have to do with anything?"

She screwed up her face. "I don't know, but I'm thinking." She ran along the beach, twisting the cord holder in her hand, trying to make her kite do something fancy, but it merely hovered high over the dunes, held aloft by the brisk breeze from the Gulf off Padre Island.

At Sunny's insistence, they had driven over thirty miles from Malaquite Beach, down the long, skinny island. The whirling in her solar plexus and the ripples down her spine had become stronger and stronger as they drove. Since Kale had seemed to be growing impatient to stop and try out their kites, she'd finally suggested that they pull over, declaring this the perfect spot. It hadn't really been her destination.

She shaded her eyes and looked southward. Her sense of distance wasn't as lousy as Kale thought. She estimated the target to be about another fifteen or twenty miles.

Gazing over the beautiful dunes that stood like sentinels along the coast, she watched a clump of sea oats ripple with the wind and a gray gull wheel and ride the currents. Sandpipers scampered along the water's edge, poking the sand with their long bills, hunting a meal. She felt sad, wondering if they would survive. She sighed. Even so, better here than centered in a more populated area. It was going to be bad enough as it was.

She let the kite string slip through her fingers.

"Sunny!" Kale made a grab for the weighted end of the cord, capturing it as it skittered along the sand.

"Whoops," she said, trying to make light of it.

"Honey, is something wrong? You look about a million miles away."

"No, only about fifteen."

He frowned. "What are you talking about?"

"The center of the hurricane is going to hit about fifteen miles south of here, maybe twenty, just north of Port Mansfield."

"What hurricane?"

"Chloe. The tropical storm we've been watching. It's going to intensify into a hurricane and hit the coast a week from today. Thank God she'll come ashore in a sparsely populated area. Corpus

Christi and Brownsville will be spared a direct hit, but the wind and water damage will be severe."

He tried to hide his skepticism, but she knew him well enough by now to recognize the subtle signs. "Are you sure?" he asked.

"Ninety-nine and forty-four-one-hundredths percent sure. I can be more accurate as the time draws closer." She tried to explain how she knew, but the whole thing sounded sort of nebulous, even to her. She was painfully aware that he was having a hard time buying the swirling in her solar plexus.

"Maybe you're just hungry. Why don't we have lunch?"

She sighed and agreed.

Kale took in the kites while she fixed their food. They sat on a beach blanket spread over the sand.

While she picked at her lunch, Sunny considered her alternatives. Knowing that she had no choice, she said, "I suppose we'd better get back to the city as soon as possible. I'll have to call the mayor so he can begin preparations. The festival will have to be postponed. Evacuation plans must be considered. The utility companies will have to be alerted."

He was quiet for a moment, his elbows propped on his knees and his fingers laced together, staring at an empty place between his feet. She could see internal struggle etched on his face. Finally, he said, "Sweetheart, don't you think it's too early to make that sort of commitment? Hundreds of thousands of dollars are at stake here."

"And you're afraid I'll be making a fool of myself?"

He only ran his fingers through his hair.

"Don't you think that I realize the position I'm putting myself in? If I go public with my prediction, I know that I'm risking making a laughing-stock of myself. Don't you think I'm agonizing about that? But if you're concerned about hundreds of thousands of dollars if I'm wrong, I'm more worried about the millions of dollars of damage that will be done if I'm right. I'm concerned about injuries and the loss of human life. Both people and property can be saved if preparations are made. Do you know the devastation that a hurricane can bring?"

A pained expression contorted his face. "More than you can imagine. I've seen Bangladesh after a typhoon. It was hell."

"Will you support me in this? Further, will KRIP support me? If not, I'll resign. I don't want to embarrass you or the station, but I have to follow my conscience." She waited for what seemed like an eternity for his answer.

More than anything, Kale wished he could take her in his arms, smooth away the worry lines in her forehead, and tell her without a qualm that he was one hundred percent behind her. He wanted to believe that she was right. The problem was that he had reservations. This new twist was infinitely more critical than a rain shower.

He'd worked his tail off trying to get KRIP back on track. Now that things were turning around, could he risk the station's credibility by supporting Sunny's outrageous prediction? KRIP might go down the tubes if she was wrong. He shuddered when he thought of the livelihoods at stake, the lawsuits sure to be filed. Foster would have a fit.

Hell, not even the leading meteorologists and hurricane specialists would venture to predict a hurricane's path with assurances of accuracy more than twenty-four to forty-eight hours in advance. Even then, they hemmed and hawed and spoke in probabilities. And this storm wasn't a hurricane yet.

He'd never put much stock in anything he couldn't see with his own eyes or hear with his own ears. He was a pragmatist, pure and simple. But when he looked into the beautiful blue eyes of the woman he loved, he saw something in their depths that made him want to take the risks involved. He had to have faith in her or lose her.

He reached over and cupped her sweet face in his callused hand and smiled. "Let's go talk to the mayor."

Laughing, Sunny threw her arms around him and toppled him in the sand. "Oh, Kale, I love you."

He laughed as she rained kisses over his face. "You picked a hell of a time to tell me."

"Do you think he believed me?" Sunny asked as they walked to the car from Mayor Garza's house.

"I think *he* believed you, all right. Remember his daughter's wedding fiasco? And his wife thinks you're a saint since you were the only forecaster along the coast who predicted that freeze last winter and she saved her precious potted plants. The question is, will the other city officials go along with him? And can he convince the mayor of Brownsville to prepare as well?"

Sunny felt as tightly wound as an old-fashioned alarm clock during the drive home. "Do you think we should go by the station and prepare an announcement for the news tonight?"

"Let's wait until tomorrow evening. That will give Mayor Garza some time to garner support. And by that time, the storm will have turned into a hurricane as you predicted and you'll have more credibility. At this point, will one day matter?"

Anger flashed through her, and she said sharply, "Sounds to me like you're trying to cover your—"

"Dammit, Sunny, be reasonable. I've told you that I'm sticking with you on this. Give me time to talk to Foster as well. He owns half the station."

"Sorry. I'm edgy."

He squeezed her thigh and patted it. "I know, honey. We both are. And I suspect that it's going to get worse. What you need now is a nice bubble bath in that tub of Ravinia's and a glass of wine. I'll wash your back." He grinned.

"I seem to remember hearing those words before." She smiled. "It sounds heavenly."

It was.

By Sunday evening, Sunny was a wreck. Kale had done everything he could to alleviate her stress, including taking her sailing on Laguna Madre that day. He had been a dear, tried to keep her spirits up, but nothing had helped. She was about to put it all on the line, and she knew it.

She had written her script carefully, but still her knees knocked and her palms sweated. She wiped her hands on her thighs and took a seat behind the news desk during the commercial break.

When the floor director cued her, she smiled faintly into the camera. "Good evening. This is Sunny Larkin with a special announcement that concerns the safety and welfare of our community.

"As you heard earlier in the program from our weekend weather reporter, Tom Crockett, tropical storm Chloe has passed over the Lesser Antilles and is now south of Puerto Rico. Only moments ago, the National Hurricane Center in Miami upgraded the storm to a hurricane, as I forecast on Friday. Although I have no desire to alarm you, I believe that the storm will intensify and enter the Gulf of Mexico." She took a deep breath.

"Neither the National Hurricane Center nor the National Weather Service will be likely to issue hurricane watches or warnings for several days, but I predict that Hurricane Chloe will make landfall on the Texas coast early Saturday morning, a few miles north of Port Mansfield. I urge everyone in our coastal viewing area, from Brownsville and Port Isabel up to Rockport and the lower end of Matagorda Island, to be on the alert and to begin all necessary precautions. This includes Corpus Christi and the surrounding area. Stay tuned to KRIP for updates on the storm's progress."

The moment the floor director signaled that the broadcast had ended, she laid her head on the desk and took deep breaths to quell the nausea.

"Sweetheart, you did fine. Just fine." Kale rubbed her back and spoke soothing words to her.

She sat up and tried her best to smile. "Well, the fat's in the fire now."

The fat sure as hell is in the fire, Kale thought as he read the Monday morning *Caller-Times*. The headline read: "PROPHECY OR PUBLICITY STUNT?" In fairness, he had to admit that the article about Sunny's hurricane forecast was handled reasonably objectively. But it looked bad. He hated for her to read it.

The phone rang and Kale snatched it up quickly, hoping that it hadn't disturbed Sunny, who needed another hour or two of sleep. It was

Foster, and his voice was an octave higher than normal.

"You've got to get to the station right away," Foster said. "All hell's breaking loose down here."

Ten

When the phone rang for the dozenth time on Wednesday morning, Sunny considered not answering it, but she couldn't abide ringing phones. She picked it up and said, "Hello."

"Well, roomie, it looks like you're famous," Estella said. "I heard your name on *Good Morning USA* a couple of hours ago—a promo for an interview tomorrow morning."

"You and most of America. My parents called from Louisiana first, then three of my brothers and sisters, and everybody else who has this supposedly unlisted number. I didn't realize that program was so popular, or that I'd become so infamous. I'm right up there with the tabloid stars like the three-headed pig sired by the man in Arkansas and the woman who murdered her husband with laxatives. I'm expecting a call from Oprah or Geraldo any moment."

Estella laughed. "What in the world is going on?"

Sunny explained about the hurricane prediction. "City government is in an uproar, but thank

goodness they decided to postpone the festival—
though not without a fight. Since the wire services
got hold of the story, the station has become a
madhouse. Kooks are coming out of the wood-
work, and reporters from all over the country have
been calling. People think I'm Kreskin. The
switchboard is suffering meltdown. I finally decided to do an interview with *Good Morning USA*.
They're sending down a crew from New York this
afternoon to do the live feed-in tomorrow morning.
They'll be staying until the storm hits—hoping,
I'm sure, that I'll make a jackass of myself."

"You won't, sweetie."

"Thanks, friend," Sunny said. "That means a
lot."

"How's Kale talking this?"

"Better than I expected. He scowls and growls
almost continuously, and lately his language
could blister the paint off the Harbor Bridge, but
he's been very supportive and protective of me.
Everybody at KRIP has rallied around. That helps.
One of the radio stations in town is taking a poll of
whether people believe me or not."

"How's it going?"

"The last I heard, about sixty–forty, pro Sunny.
I'm not sure how scientific it is. Kale and Hulon
called in about five times each."

"How'd they vote?"

Sunny laughed. "Pro, I hope. I voted twice myself." She paused, then said, "I wish you were
here. You have a way of keeping things in perspec-
tive. I miss you."

"I can be there in a shot if you need me," Estella
said.

"Thanks, but you need to be tending Eddie.
How *is* my godson, by the way?"

"Growing like a weed. And his daddy will be

home in two weeks. I bought a sexy new night-gown for the occasion."

"Better watch out or Eddie will have a new little brother or sister before his first birthday."

"Bite your tongue, girl," Estella said. "How did your special on gangs go? Have you finished it?"

"Yes. It aired Monday evening to good reviews, but with all the hoopla about the hurricane, it was sort of anticlimactic. I was sorry about the timing. I worked hard on that piece, and I'm very proud of it."

Sunny and Estella chatted for a few minutes longer, then said their good-byes. It had felt great to discuss normal things for a change.

Late Wednesday night Sunny sat in Ravinia's tub, sipping a glass of wine. Kale sat behind her, kneading the tension from her neck and shoulders. She closed her eyes and moaned.

"Feel good?" he asked, working his thumbs down her spine.

"Delicious. Absolutely delicious. I may keep you, just for your hands. This has been a horrendous day, but I have the feeling that it's going to get much worse before this thing is over."

"Umm-hmm." He trailed a line of kisses along the back of her neck. "I had the yard man put up the storm shutters today and store the patio furniture and hanging baskets in the garage. Did you notice?"

"No, but thanks for the vote of confidence."

He wrapped his arms around her, pulled her back against him, and rubbed the roughness of his cheek against the softness of hers. "Chloe has done everything you've said she would. Anybody would be a fool to doubt you."

"I only hope we can convince everyone. When the skies are clear and the sun is shining, it's hard to persuade folks to leave their homes. But if the ones living in low-lying areas haven't evacuated by Friday, they'll be stranded. The people on Padre and some of the other islands will be cut off by high tides."

"The mayor is doing what he can. And the president of the Chamber of Commerce is firmly in your corner. The schools will be closed Friday. That's good."

"I know," she said. "Could we talk about something else? I'd like to forget about Chloe for a little while."

"Did I ever tell you how beautiful your eyes are? They remind me of a very special taw I had as a kid."

She laughed as she climbed out of the tub and reached for a towel. "My eyes remind you of a marble?"

"Let me do that," he said, taking the towel from her and rubbing her dry with long, sensuous strokes. "Mind you, this wasn't just any marble. It was a honey of a shooter. As clear and blue as the Mediterranean—though I'd never seen the Mediterranean at the time. I could knock anything out of the ring with that taw. I was convinced that it was magic. I was the marble terror of Tenaha, Texas, and I always ended up with a pocketful of agates."

She looped a towel around his neck, pulled his face down to hers, and gave him a quick kiss. "I had you pegged as a hustler. You started young."

"A hustler? Me? Woman, you wound me. Take that back."

"Nope," she said saucily. "I calls 'em like I sees 'em, Mr. Network Stud."

"That's worse. If you don't take it back, I'll have to resort to drastic measures." He grinned.

Her eyes widened and she batted her lashes. "*Drastic* measures? I'm quaking in my boots."

"You ticklish?" He reached for her rib cage, and she scooted backward, protecting her sides with her elbows.

"Kale Hoaglin! Don't you dare. You know I am."

"Take it back?"

"Nooooo," she shrieked, wiggling away from his tickling. She bolted from Ravinia's room, laughing as she slammed the door behind her. She sprinted to her bedroom, turned the lock, and leaned against the door.

"I've got you now, Miss Smart Mouth," Kale said, grinning as he came through the connecting bath.

Sunny dashed across the room, putting the bed between them. She snatched up a pillow as he advanced on her. "Don't you dare tickle me, Kale Hoaglin. That's cruel and unusual punishment."

He only grinned wider, wiggled his eyebrows, and kept coming. Shrieking with laughter, she leaped on the bed and whopped him with the pillow. He grabbed another pillow, jumped on the bed, and whopped her in retaliation. They beat on each other like two kids at a slumber party, laughing too hard to do any harm.

Suddenly the bed gave way with a crash, and they fell in a tumble of arms and legs on the mattress, which tilted at an odd angle.

"Ooops!" she said between giggles.

Before she could move, Kale captured her wrists and straddled her body. "You going to retract that crack?"

A bubble of laughter exploded in her throat.

"Mr. Network Stud, you're not only a hustler, but a bad poet."

"That tears it." His lips took hers in an open-mouthed kiss so potent that her whole body went on standby alert and her toes curled. She tried to move her arms to put them around him, but he held her fast. "Uh-uh," he murmured as he moved down her body to lave and suckle her breasts. "I'm going to torture you, make love to you until you say 'uncle.'"

He nudged her knees apart and moved between them, then circled her navel with the tip of his tongue. He moved lower and lower until her eyes widened. "Kale!"

He looked up at her and chuckled. "Row four." Then he lifted her hips to lave and nip her most sensitive of spots. Soon she was writhing under his ministrations. She hadn't realized her hands were free until she grabbed handfuls of his hair when the pleasure grew too much to bear. His attentions continued until she sucked in a deep breath and contracted her back as wave after wave of delicious sensation engulfed her.

She went limp as a dishrag. "Uncle," she whispered listlessly.

"Too late," he said, starting again.

Much later, they lay in Kale's bed, bodies damp from lovemaking. Sunny yawned as she stroked his chest. "Whatever happened to your blue marble?"

"I think Billy Wanamaker stole it. I could never prove it, but I'm sure he did. He's a state senator now."

"Figures." Totally relaxed, she smiled and nestled in the peaceful comfort of his arms, wishing she could stay there forever.

Sunny was anything but relaxed. Jessica Martin of *Good Morning USA*, for all her surface charm, was a tough interviewer. But Sunny expected no less; she was tough herself. She was determined to appear cool and professional.

"I understand," Jessica said, "that on Tuesday night you made certain predictions about the approaching hurricane. What were those predictions?"

"I stated that Chloe would pass over the western tip of Cuba, stall, intensify to a category three hurricane, and then move in a westerly direction."

"And what happened?"

"It acted exactly as I predicted. Yesterday at six o'clock, the National Hurricane Center declared Chloe a category three hurricane with a tightly defined eye and winds of one hundred and twenty-five miles per hour. After having stalled for several hours, it is now moving slowly in a westerly direction, approximately seven hundred and fifty miles southeast of Corpus Christi, Texas."

"And you believe that it will hit Corpus Christi?"

"No, not directly. The eye will move over an area to the south of us, but Corpus Christi and the surrounding areas will feel the effects and can expect extremely high winds and heavy rain, and tides will run six or seven feet above normal. Our weather will be severe and damaging."

"You say this will happen on Saturday?" Jessica asked, one eyebrow slightly askew.

"Yes. It will begin moving ashore shortly before dawn."

"Tell me, Sunny—" Jessica leaned toward her,

and Sunny thought, *Uh-oh, here it comes.* "Tell me how you can predict the path of a hurricane when it befuddles our finest scientists. Are you a witch?"

Sunny turned her most engaging smile on the camera. "No. I don't ride a broomstick." She chuckled. "I don't even own a cat. I'm simply an ordinary person with an odd quirk to her nature—a talent, some would say, like having a green thumb or being able to fix mechanical things. I can predict the weather that affects the area where I am."

"And you're always right?"

"Always." Sunny chose to ignore the single miss when she'd had the flu.

Jessica turned to the camera and smiled. "And there you have it. We've been talking to Sunny Larkin, evening news anchor for KRIP-TV in Corpus Christi, Texas, who is defying science and predicting the course of the hurricane in the Gulf of Mexico. Back to you in New York, John."

Sunny's blue silk blouse was decidedly damp under the arms when they finished, but when she glanced at Kale, he gave her a thumbs-up and winked. She smiled, then made polite remarks to Jessica and escaped with the excuse that she had work to do.

Kale met her in the hall and they went downstairs to his office. When the door was closed, she melted into a chair. "Whew! That lady has sharp teeth."

"She's what you can expect if you want to swim with the network sharks."

"I think I held my own pretty well."

"You were fantastic," he said. "Made old Jessica look like an amateur."

"I don't believe a word of it, but you do wonders for my ego, Mr. Hoaglin."

"And you do wonders for my libido, Miss Larkin. Come here." He pulled her to her feet and kissed her, a long, lingering kiss that pushed everything out of her head. Until his phone rang.

"Hold my place," he said, tapping her lips.

"I really do have work to do. I'll see you later."

The rest of the day was hectic, spent primarily in the newsroom, tracking the hurricane on radar and preparing for the periodic updates and the evening news.

Experts from the National Hurricane Center said that assuming Chloe turned north, as was characteristic of hurricanes, she might make landfall along the upper Texas or Louisiana coast. Corpus Christi was on the outermost fringe of their probability table. Assuming. Maybe. Perhaps. Might. If. But. The experts gave a thousand qualifiers. Sunny knew exactly.

On Friday morning, Sunny, her arms hugged tightly under her breasts, stood at the window of her fourth-floor office and stared at the bay. The sun shone; the water was calm; it was a beautiful day. Despondency filled her so completely that her bones ached. Kale stood beside her, his arm around her shoulders.

"Cheer up, honey," Kale said. "I don't like to see you like this."

"Cheer up? Only moments ago, Jessica Martin chewed me up and spit me out. She made me look like a fool. Several million people across the country now think I'm a raving lunatic."

During the night, Chloe had stumbled once or twice, then veered north. Experts had sucked in their guts and declared that there was a fifty percent chance that the hurricane would make landfall around midnight near Galveston. Corpus wasn't in the range of probability.

Kale hugged Sunny to him. "By this time tomorrow Jessica Martin will be eating her words. Better yet, around midnight we'll chain her ankle to one of the lampposts on the jetty and, come morning, Chloe will give her the thrashing she deserves."

Sunny laughed and buried her nose against his chest. "What would I do without you?"

"I've been trying to tell you that I'm indispensable. If I weren't around, who would keep you out of mischief? Who would find your car keys?"

She looked up at him. "What if I'm wrong, Kale? What if I'm wrong?"

"You're not wrong, sweetheart." He wrapped his arms around her and squeezed her close. "Get that idea out of your head. Don't let those cynical bastards get you down."

She chuckled. "You've come a long way in a few weeks. You were the world-champion cynic. I'm glad you believe in me." Turning in his arms until she faced the window again, she added, "And I'm glad they do."

She pointed to city crews working along the wide earth median of Shoreline Drive. Huge holes had been dug in the divider with backhoes, and they were burying boats from the marina. The harbor was almost empty. Those vessels too big to bury or haul easily had been moved or triple-tied. The barge restaurant where Sunny and Kale often ate had been towed up the ship channel to a safer port.

Windows were being boarded up, loose material

nailed down, and evacuation was proceeding as planned. Foster had sent his family to Austin on Thursday. Emergency supplies were being stockpiled, and grocery stores were running low on bread and nonperishable items. Sterno, candles, and flashlights were gone from the shelves, and batteries were at a premium.

The station was fully stocked; cartons lined the walls, filled with everything that could conceivably be needed. Kale had taken care of that. The emergency generators had been checked so that KRIP could stay on the air unless the tower went down, which was likely.

Roland Cantu and a camera crew were about to leave for Port Mansfield. Tom Crockett and another crew were en route to Brownsville, and two additional teams had been dispatched to Rockport and Galveston. The other KRIP employees had brought cots, sleeping bags and clothes to the station, prepared to settle in for the duration.

"I should be going to Port Mansfield instead of Roland," Sunny said.

Kale's arms tightened around her. "I've told you that I absolutely forbid it."

Sunny sighed, not wanting to reopen that argument, and rapped on the window with her knuckles. "Think this will hold?"

"It should. Foster assured me that Aunt Ravinia had only the best installed. They're special storm windows—tempered safety glass, guaranteed."

"It seems that you've thought of everything. What do we do now?"

"Now, love," he said, resting his chin atop her head, "we wait."

• • •

At six-fifteen, during a commercial on the evening news, an assistant laid a piece of paper on Sunny's desk.

When the break was over, the camera cut to Sunny, who said, "I have this bulletin just in from the National Weather Service. Hurricane Chloe has stalled in the Gulf." She read the coordinates giving the longitude and latitude. "This puts her center approximately two hundred miles east-southeast of Corpus Christi."

At eight-thirty, with the remnants of their Chinese dinner in little boxes on Kale's desk, Sunny sat curled up in his lap, drawing strength from him. He held her firmly, quietly, undemandingly as they waited.

She felt as if she were in limbo, helpless to do anything but anticipate the approaching onslaught with dread. It occurred to her that waiting for the storm was analogous to waiting for the day of Kale's leaving. Although he hadn't mentioned it to her, scuttlebutt had it that Kale's bureau chief had called twice in the past week urging him back to his post. The dreaded events were both coming closer and closer. Inevitable. Uncontrollable. Devastating.

She snuggled into the perfect cradle of his arms, her hand on his chest, feeling the beat of his heart beneath her fingers, breathing his familiar spicy scent. She hadn't intended to fall in love with him, but she had. How would she deal with the hole he would leave in her life?

After hurricanes passed, people rebuilt and went on with their lives, but there were always scars gouged in the land that took years and years to heal. Even then, things were never quite the same again.

"You're awfully quiet," Kale said.

Pain slashed through her as she looked up at his dear face. She stroked his jaw—relaxed now rather than perpetually clenched, as it had been only weeks ago—and felt the faint stubble of his beard. "I love you," she whispered. "Remember that."

"I love you, too, sweetheart." He kissed her tenderly.

At a quarter of ten, Sunny ripped a page off the printer. Her stomach churning and shivers rippling up her back like a frightened snake, she turned to Kale with anxious eyes.

"She's moving again. Fast. She's changed direction and is headed our way."

At one o'clock, Kale insisted that Sunny try to get an hour or two's rest, promising that he'd take over the half-hour updates himself.

At one-thirty, Sunny was back on the job.

At two A.M., KRIP ran an old Humphrey Bogart movie. Only a shift worker in Refugio called to complain when they interrupted the film frequently with the latest news of Chloe inching her way westward on the radar screen.

By four o'clock Sunny and Kale were on the air almost constantly, working as an efficient reporting team.

Shortly before dawn, the winds picked up and the rains began as the outer bands of thunderstorms started moving ashore.

"Hold the fort," Sunny said to Kale during a

break for a report from one of the field teams. "I'm going outside with Carlos to get some shots."

"Like hell you will! You're staying in here. I'll go outside with Carlos."

"Like hell I am!" She jacked up her chin and glared at him. "This is *my* story."

He chuckled and kissed her pursed lips. "Then we'll both go. Hulon! Come here and take over for a few minutes."

Hulon, his bow tie askew and his toupee ruffled, looked horrified, but he scurried to the desk when Kale barked the order.

Dressing quickly in boots and raincoats with hoods, the trio went downstairs to the seawall. Wind whipped at their clothes and rain stung their faces. The sky had lightened only slightly. Dark clouds obscured the rising sun, and haloed street lamps struggled to provide illumination through the downpour. Pitching waves battered the curving, lighted jetty, smashing against the huge rocks and sending high sprays dashing over the sidewalk along the top.

They filmed for a few minutes, yelling into their mikes to be heard. When the wind intensified so that Sunny had to hold on to Kale to stand up, he dragged her back inside.

After drying off quickly, they were back behind the desk. The roaring of wind and water grew louder, and the lights flickered, then died. The generator immediately took over, providing emergency power. Their broadcast continued as walls creaked and windows rattled.

"The tower is down!" Foster yelled. "We're off the air."

Repair crews had been dispatched, but until Chloe's fury abated as she moved over land, nothing much could be done.

Kale rose, took Sunny's hand, and said, "That's it for a while. You're exhausted. Let's go down to my office and get some rest."

Jessica Martin, looking considerably worse than she did when she'd bustled into the station around midnight, trailed behind them, gushing. "Oh, what a story! This is fantastic. Sunny, could I have just a few words with you?"

His jaw clenched and his eyes as cold as an Arctic winter, Kale looked the reporter up and down. "Miss Martin . . . go to hell."

On Sunday, cleanup began. With Chloe's main fury spent and her ragged remnants drifting through central Texas, the encroaching waters slipped back into the Gulf, uncovering the T-Heads and L-Heads and receding from the road-ways. The KRIP tower was repaired, and utility crews worked feverishly trying to restore power and services to the area. Storm windows came down and plywood sheets were stored or trashed. Insurance agents went to work, and pots of red geraniums went back to sitting on porches.

At the breakfast table, Kale proudly held up the front page of the *Caller-Times*. The banner head-line read simply: THANKS, SUNNY! She laughed.

"About damned time they learned to appreciate you," Kale said, dropping a kiss on her nose. "There was some serious property damage, but not a single life was lost."

By Monday, although some repairs would take weeks to complete, most things were back to normal. Cleanup continued, but Mother Nature, as penance for birthing Chloe, had bestowed sun-shine and a cool breeze to dry out the city.

Sunny was sitting at her desk working when the

phone rang. She hesitated to answer it. The blasted thing had been ringing like mad since she'd come in, and she had a stack of message slips an inch thick. Oprah and Geraldo—or, rather, their producers—*had* called.

She reluctantly picked up the phone. It was an agent trying to hustle her, promising big bucks for appearances and maybe even a book. She told him thanks, but no thanks, and hung up.

The darned thing rang again almost immediately. She snatched it up and said a grumpy, "Hello."

When the caller identified himself as William Hix, a vice president of the network, she sat up straight. As she listened to him, her heart began to beat faster and a smile spread across her face. "Yes, Mr. Hix, I'm very interested. May I get back to you in a few days?"

After the conversation ended, she sat stunned for a moment, the receiver still glued to her ear. When the buzz of the dial tone broke through her stupor, she hung up, flung out her arms, and yelled, "Whoopee!"

Startled when the door banged open, Kale smiled when he saw Sunny. Her eyes shone like sparkling blue crystals, and her dimples were deeply etched in her cheeks from a bubbling smile that warmed him from across the room.

"Have I got news for you!" she said, laughing and turning in circles. "Guess who just called me."

He caught her hand and pulled her into his lap. "The Queen of England."

She rested her forehead against his and rubbed his nose with hers. "Nope. Guess again."

"Elvis."

She laughed. "No. William Hix, a vice president of the network, called me from New York."

She looked excited enough to explode, and so adorable that he wanted to wrap her up and put her in his pocket. "I see," he drawled. "And what did old Bill have to say?"

"He said that he thought I was the greatest thing since sliced bread—or words to that effect—and that I'd done a 'damned fine job' with the hurricane story. He also said that he'd seen my special on gangs and that it was 'an *excellent* piece of work.' Aaaand," she added, drawing out the word for dramatic impact, "he offered me a job at the Washington Bureau." She squealed and laughed and kissed his face all over.

Kale joined in her laughter, delighting in her excitement. "That's great, love. Just great."

Sunny cocked her head and drew her eyebrows together. "I wonder how Mr. Hix knew about the gang special?"

"Maybe a little bird sent him a copy of the tape."

Her eyes narrowed and a smile played at the corner of her delectable mouth. "Are *you* the little bird?" She poked him in the ribs.

"Naw. It must have been Hulon." He was about to kiss away her questions when the phone rang. He punched the button to activate the speaker-phone, and barked, "Hoaglin."

"Hoaglin," a gruff voice bellowed, "you've pussy-footed around with that two-bit station in Texas long enough. All hell is breaking loose in Tel Aviv. Kiss that little piece you're shacked up with good-bye and get your tail on a plane—"

Kale disconnected the speaker, but he could see that the damage had been done. The happy ani-mation had drained from Sunny's face, and she looked stricken. She flew from his lap and tore out of the room with him calling after her.

"Goddamn it, Stan Verick," Kale roared, "if I could get my hands on you, I'd ring your scrawny neck!" Still cursing, he slammed the receiver down so hard that the plastic cracked. He grabbed something from his desk drawer and ran from his office, looking for Sunny.

She had disappeared.

He looked everywhere he could think of, twice. He'd checked outside first, but she wasn't in sight. Her little red car was in the lot, so she had to be in the building. But, dammit, where?

He went back upstairs and stuck his nose in every office. He even looked in the ladies' room and the broom closet. Where had she gone? He tried to think. When an idea hit him, he strode to the end of the newsroom and stuck his head out the window.

There she sat. On the ledge. Scrunched up in a little ball in the far corner.

"Dammit, Sunny, what are you doing out there?"

She glared at him. "Would you please stop saying, 'Dammit, Sunny.' My first name is not *dammit*. You need to watch your language. You have an absolutely foul mouth."

"Yes, ma'am. Sunny, my precious, my love, what in the hell are you doing out there?"

"I'm sitting here being miserable. Go away."

He kicked off his loafers and climbed out on the ledge with her. He sat down close to her and swung his legs over the edge.

"Be careful," she said. "You're going to fall off and break your neck."

"Naw. I'm resilient. I'd probably bounce." He glanced at her from the corner of his eye. She wasn't laughing. In fact, he saw that her lashes were clumped with moisture and that there were salty tear streaks on her cheeks. Pain pierced his gut, and he grew angry with Stan all over again. "Sweetheart, forget what Stan Verick said. He's a nasty-minded bastard who's got rocks for brains. He's not worth being miserable over. He doesn't even know about you. He was just shooting off his mouth."

She wiped her nose with the back of her hand. He fished his handkerchief from his rear pocket and held it to her nose. "Blow."

She made a big honking noise. "Thanks." She sighed and clutched her knees tightly to her chest. "It's not just what he said." She fluttered her hand. "It's everything."

"But, honey, you were so happy. You were thrilled about the job offer in Washington. It's what you've always wanted, isn't it?"

"Yes, but—" Her face screwed up and tears started rolling again.

It nearly killed him to see her cry. He scooted closer and lifted her face. "But what, love?"

"But you're going to Tel Aviv, and I'll probably never see you again," she wailed, the tears coming faster.

He wanted to take her into his arms, but they would probably fall off the damned ledge if he tried. "I'm not going to Tel Aviv."

Her eyes widened. "You're not?"

"Nope." He reached into the pocket of his pink shirt, pulled out a small velvet box, and opened it. "I meant to pick a more romantic spot to do this, but will you marry me?"

Her eyes grew even wider. "But, Kale, how can we get married?"

"The usual way. You buy a pretty dress, and I'll

buy you some flowers. How about we book one of the Miradores for the ceremony? We'll find a preacher and—"

"No, no. How can we get married if I'm going to be in Washington and you're going to be Lord knows where most of the time? No matter what Estella says, I don't think that's much of a marriage. I—"

He put his finger over her lips. "Love, I'm not going to be 'Lord knows where.' My globe-trotting days are over. I'm going to be wherever you are. If you want to stay here, we'll stay here. If you want to take the job in Washington, I'll go with you. Just give me a couple of weeks to hire a new anchor for KRIP. After our honeymoon—how does Greece sound?—we can find a nice little town house in Georgetown and—"

"What would you do in Washington? For a job, I mean."

He laughed. "I'm not exactly destitute. Ravinia left Foster and me enough money to last four lifetimes. And I've been thinking that I might write a book. I have an editor friend who's been hounding me about the idea for a couple of years."

"But I thought you loved being a foreign correspondent."

"I thought so, too, until I had a chance to get away from it. I've had my fill of the cesspools of the earth. I've resigned. You've opened a whole new world for me, Sunny Larkin, and I'm not about to let go of it. I love you, sweetheart. Will you marry me?"

The sunlight came back into her eyes, and her dimples deepened with a dazzling smile. "I will." She held out her hand.

When he slipped the diamond solitaire on her

finger, the stone seemed to wink at them in the bright daylight.

"Dammit, Sunny, let's get off this ledge," he said. "I want to kiss you properly."

She laughed. "Some things never change. But I love you anyway."

They climbed inside to find a dozen pairs of eyes staring at them.

"We're engaged," Kale announced with a grin.

A beaming Hulon led the applause.

Before the group could descend on them, Kale dragged Sunny to her small office and firmly shut the door. "Now I want to kiss my fiancée."

"Kale, are you very sure that this is what you want?"

"To kiss you? Damned sure."

"No, I mean are you sure you want to resign from your job?"

"Positive. I faxed my resignation first thing this morning. I would have done it sooner, but, as you recall, things have been a little hectic around here."

She looked puzzled. "Then why did your boss call today?"

"Because Stan is a stubborn old coot who doesn't understand about love and marriage. But, for me, the choice between going back to my old life and having you was no contest."

She frowned. "I don't want you to make a decision because of me that you'll regret one day. Maybe we could work out some other arrangement."

He shook his head. "Sweetheart, I'm burned out. I have been for a couple of years, but I didn't have the sense to recognize it. You made me aware of what a damned mess I was in. I'd forgotten how to laugh, how to feel, until I met you. I can walk away with no regrets. And the idea of writing a book appeals to me. I can write anywhere, so we'll move where your opportunity is. With me around to find your car keys and give you baths, you're going to be the best damned reporter Washington, D.C., has ever seen. You'll wow 'em."

Eyes shining and that fantastic smile turned on high, she stood on tiptoes and offered her lips. He kissed her with all the love that was in him.

THE EDITOR'S CORNER

There are certain stories we all know and love, whether they're fairy tales, classic novels, or unforgettable plays. We treasure them for the way they touch our heart and soul, make us laugh or cry—or both—and next month LOVESWEPT presents you with a bounty of **TREASURED TALES,** six wonderful romances inspired by beloved stories. With special messages from the authors and gorgeous covers featuring black-and-white photographs that reflect the timelessness of these stories, **TREASURED TALES** are worth a king's ransom!

Starting the lineup is Helen Mittermeyer with **'TWAS THE NIGHT,** LOVESWEPT #588, a stirring version of **BEAUTY AND THE BEAST**. It was on Christmas Eve that Rafe Brockman and Cassie Nordstrom first met, but then they parted as enemies. Now, years later, fate brings them together again on Christmas Eve, and they learn that the gift of love is the true Christmas miracle. A heartwarming story from one of the genre's most popular authors.

In **THE PRINCESS AND THE PEA,** LOVESWEPT #589, Fayrene Preston gives her heroine something more intriguing—and gorgeous—to deal with than a troublesome legume. Though Cameron Tate is the perfect hunk to star in a jeans commercial, all Melisande Lanier wants from him is his bed. But Cameron will sell only if workaholic Mel slows down long enough to fall in love with him. Fayrene's winning charm makes this enchanting story shine.

Like Sydney Carton in Charles Dickens's *A Tale of Two Cities,* Nick Atwell is a rebel with a taste for trouble, but his **RENEGADE WAYS,** LOVESWEPT #590 by Terry

Lawrence, can't dissuade Connie Hennessy from believing the handsome diplomat might be just the hero she needs. And she quickly lets Nick know she's willing to barter heated kisses for Nick's help in a perilous mission. Terry really lets the sparks fly between these two characters.

With **NIGHT DREAMS,** LOVESWEPT #591, Sandra Chastain gives us a hero as unforgettable as the Phantom from *The Phantom of the Opera*. No one knows the truth behind the legend of Jonathan Dream, the playboy who'd vanished after building an empire. But when Shannon Summers is taken to his castle to help his disabled daughter, she learns of his scars and his secrets—and burns with the wildfire of his desire. Sandra tells this story with stunning force.

Snow White was contented living with the seven dwarfs, but in **THE FAIREST OF THEM ALL** by Leanne Banks, LOVESWEPT #592, Carly Pendleton would like nothing better than for her seven loving, but overbearing brothers to let her have her own life. Longtime friend Russ Bradford agrees, especially since he has plans to claim her for his own and to taste the sweetness of her ruby-red lips. Leanne delivers a wonderfully entertaining read.

Peggy Webb will light up your day with **DARK FIRE,** LOVESWEPT #593. Although Sid Granger isn't as short on looks as Cyrano de Bergerac, he doesn't dare court the beautiful Rose Anne Jones because he thinks he can never match her perfection. Instead he agrees to woo her for a friend, but the thought of her in another man's arms sends the fighter pilot soaring to her side. Peggy has once again created an irresistible, sensuous romance.

On sale this month are four fabulous FANFARE titles. From *New York Times* bestselling author Amanda Quick comes **RECKLESS,** a tale of a tarnished knight, a daring maiden, and a sweet, searing, storybook love. When

Phoebe Layton needs help to carry out a quest, she can imagine no one more suited to the job than Gabriel Banner. But the Earl of Wylde has a quest of his own in mind: to possess Phoebe, heart and soul.

The Delaneys are here with **THE DELANEY CHRIST-MAS CAROL!** For this long-awaited addition to this enduring family's saga, Kay Hooper, Iris Johansen, and Fayrene Preston teamed up once again, and now we're thrilled to give you three tales of three generations of Delaneys in love and of the changing face of Christmas—past, present, and future. Enjoy our special holiday offer to you.

If you missed Tami Hoag's novel **SARAH'S SIN** the first time around, you can pick up a copy now and discover a warm, moving story of two cultures in conflict and two hearts in love. Matt Thorne is every fantasy Sarah Troyer has ever had. And though there's a high price to pay for giving herself to one outside the Amish ways, Sarah dares to allow herself a brief, secret adventure in the arms of a forbidden man.

Maureen Reynolds has been described by *Romantic Times* as "a very HOT writer," and the tempestuous historical romance **SMOKE EYES** will show you why. Katherine Flynn has worked hard to overcome the double prejudice she faced as a woman and an Arapaho half-breed, but she can't win against the power of desire when Zach Fletcher abruptly returns to her life.

Also on sale this month in the Doubleday hardcover edition is **CONFIDENCES** by Penny Hayden. In the tradition of Danielle Steel, **CONFIDENCES** is a deeply moving novel about four "thirty-something" mothers and a long-held secret that could save the life of a seventeen-year-old boy.

Well, folks, it's around that time of year when people usually take stock of what they've accomplished and look forward to what's ahead. And one of the things we've been taking stock of is **THE EDITOR'S CORNER**. It's been a continuing feature in LOVESWEPT books since LOVESWEPT #1 was published. That makes almost ten years' worth of previews, and we wonder if it's still something you look forward to every month, or if there's something else you'd like to see perhaps. Let us know; we'd love to hear your opinions and/or suggestions.

Happy reading!

With warmest wishes,

Nita Taublib
Associate Publisher
LOVESWEPT and FANFARE

OFFICIAL RULES TO WINNERS CLASSIC SWEEPSTAKES

No Purchase necessary. To enter the sweepstakes follow instructions found elsewhere in this offer. You can also enter the sweepstakes by hand printing your name, address, city, state and zip code on a 3" x 5" piece of paper and mailing it to: Winners Classic Sweepstakes, P.O. Box 785, Gibbstown, NJ 08027. Mail each entry separately. Sweepstakes begins 12/1/91. Entries must be received by 6/1/93. Some presentations of this sweepstakes may feature a deadline for the Early Bird prize. If the offer you receive does, then to be eligible for the Early Bird prize your entry must be received according to the Early Bird date specified. Not responsible for lost, late, damaged, misdirected, illegible or postage due mail. Mechanically reproduced entries are not eligible. All entries become property of the sponsor and will not be returned.

Prize Selection/Validations: Winners will be selected in random drawings on or about 7/30/93, by VENTURA ASSOCIATES, INC., an independent judging organization whose decisions are final. Odds of winning are determined by total number of entries received. Circulation of this sweepstakes is estimated not to exceed 200 million. Entrants need not be present to win. All prizes are guaranteed to be awarded and delivered to winners. Winners will be notified by mail and may be required to complete an affidavit of eligibility and release of liability which must be returned within 14 days of date of notification or alternate winners will be selected. Any guest of a trip winner will also be required to execute a release of liability. Any prize notification letter or any prize returned to a participating sponsor, Bantam Doubleday Dell Publishing Group, Inc., its participating divisions or subsidiaries, or VENTURA ASSOCIATES, INC. as undeliverable will be awarded to an alternate winner. Prizes are not transferable. No multiple prize winners except as may be necessary due to unavailability, in which case a prize of equal or greater value will be awarded. Prizes will be awarded approximately 90 days after the drawing. All taxes, automobile license and registration fees, if applicable, are the sole responsibility of the winners. Entry constitutes permission (except where prohibited) to use winners' names and likenesses for publicity purposes without further or other compensation.

Participation: This sweepstakes is open to residents of the United States and Canada, except for the province of Quebec. This sweepstakes is sponsored by Bantam Doubleday Dell Publishing Group, Inc. (BDD), 666 Fifth Avenue, New York, NY 10103. Versions of this sweepstakes with different graphics will be offered in conjunction with various solicitations or promotions by different subsidiaries and divisions of BDD. Employees and their families of BDD, its division, subsidiaries, advertising agencies, and VENTURA ASSOCIATES, INC., are not eligible.

Canadian residents, in order to win, must first correctly answer a time limited arithmetical skill testing question. Void in Quebec and wherever prohibited or restricted by law. Subject to all federal, state, local and provincial laws and regulations.

Prizes: The following values for prizes are determined by the manufacturers' suggested retail prices or by what these items are currently known to be selling for at the time this offer was published. Approximate retail values include handling and delivery of prizes. Estimated maximum retail value of prizes: 1 Grand Prize ($27,500 if merchandise or $25,000 Cash); 1 First Prize ($3,000); 5 Second Prizes ($400 each); 35 Third Prizes ($100 each); 1,000 Fourth Prizes ($9.00 each); 1 Early Bird Prize ($5,000); Total approximate maximum retail value is $50,000. Winners will have the option of selecting any prize offered at level won. Automobile winner must have a valid driver's license at the time the car is awarded. Trips are subject to space and departure availability. Certain black-out dates may apply. Travel must be completed within one year from the time the prize is awarded. Minors must be accompanied by an adult. Prizes won by minors will be awarded in the name of parent or legal guardian.

For a list of Major Prize Winners (available after 7/30/93): send a self-addressed, stamped envelope entirely separate from your entry to: Winners Classic Sweepstakes Winners, P.O. Box 825, Gibbstown, NJ 08027. Requests must be received by 6/1/93. DO NOT SEND ANY OTHER CORRESPONDENCE TO THIS P.O. BOX.

The Delaney Dynasty lives on in

The Delaney Christmas Carol

by Kay Hooper, Iris Johansen, &
Fayrene Preston

Three of romantic fiction's best-loved authors present the changing face of Christmas spirit—past, present, and future—as they tell the story of three generations of Delaneys in love.

<u>CHRISTMAS PAST by Iris Johansen</u>

From the moment he first laid eyes on her, Kevin Delaney felt a curious attraction for the ragclad Gypsy beauty rummaging through the attic of his ranch at Killara. He didn't believe for a moment her talk of magic mirrors and second-sight, but something about Zara St. Cloud stirred his blood. Now, as Christmas draws near, a touch leads to a kiss and a gift of burning passion.

<u>CHRISTMAS PRESENT by Fayrene Preston</u>

Bria Delaney had been looking for Christmas ornaments in her mother's attic, when she saw him in the mirror for the first time—a stunningly handsome man with sky-blue eyes and red-gold hair. She had almost convinced herself he was only a dream when Kells Braxton arrived at Killara and led them both to a holiday wonderland of sensuous pleasure.

<u>CHRISTMAS FUTURE by Kay Hooper</u>

As the last of the Delaney men, Brett returned to Killara this Christmastime only to find it in the capable hands of his father's young and beautiful widow. Yet the closer he got to Cassie, the more Brett realized that the embers of their old love still burned and that all it would take was a look, a kiss, a caress, to turn their dormant passion into an inferno.

The best in Women's Fiction from Bantam FANFARE.
On sale in November 1992   AN 428 9/92

FANFARE

On Sale in November

RECKLESS
29315-X $5.50/6.50 in Canada
by Amanda Quick
New York Times bestselling author of
RENDEZVOUS and RAVISHED

THE DELANEY CHRISTMAS CAROL
29654-X $4.99/5.99 in Canada
by Kay Hooper, Iris Johansen, and Fayrene Preston

UNSUITABLE COMPANY
29712-0 $5.99/6.99 in Canada
by Judith Green

SARAH'S SIN
56050-6 $4.50//5.50 in Canada
by Tami Hoag
author of STILL WATERS and LUCKY'S LADY

SMOKE EYES
29501-2 $4.99/5.99 in Canada
by Maureen Reynolds
"A very HOT writer." --*Romantic Times*

FANFARE

On Sale in December

THE TIGER PRINCE

☐ 29968-9 $5.50/6.50 in Canada
by Iris Johansen
Bantam's "Mistress of Romantic Fantasy"
author of THE GOLDEN BARBARIAN

LADY DEFIANT

☐ 29574-9 $4.99/5.99 in Canada
by Suzanne Robinson
Bestselling author of LADY GALLANT
and LADY HELLFIRE

"Lavish in atmosphere, rich in adventure, filled with suspense
and passion, LADY DEFIANT is a fitting sequel to
LADY GALLANT. Suzanne Robinson brilliantly captures the
era with all the intrigue, costume, drama, and romance that
readers adore." --*Romantic Times*

PRIVATE SCANDALS

☐ 56053-0 $4.99//5.99 in Canada
by Christy Cohen
A stunning debut novel of friendship,
betrayal, and passionate romance

A LOVE FOR ALL TIME

☐ 29996-4 $4.50/5.50 in Canada
by Dorothy Garlock
One of Ms. Garlock's most beloved romances of all time